LOVE AFTER

DREAMS STILL COME TRUE

RUSSELL GRAY &
MONA GUARINO

For permission requests, write to the publisher, addressed "Attention: Permissions Coordinator," carol@markvictorhansenlibrary.com

Quantity sales special discounts are available on quantity purchases by corporations, associations, and others. For details, contact the publisher at carol@markvictorhansenlibrary.com

Orders by U.S. trade bookstores and wholesalers. Email: carol@markvictorhansenlibrary.com

Creative Contribution - Tracey Bleier and Denise Long
Cover Design - Low & Joe Creative, Brea, CA 92821
Book Layout - DBree, StoneBear Design

Manufactured and printed in the United States of America distributed globally by markvictorhansenlibrary.com

MVHL

New York | Los Angeles | London | Sydney

ISBN: 979-8-88581-053-1 Hardback
ISBN: 979-8-88581-054-8 Paperback
ISBN: 979-8-88581-055-5 eBook
Library of Congress Control Number: 2022915914

THE SAVANNAH VALLEY SERIES

Everyone imagines what life will be like in retirement. Perhaps you know someone who ended up in a depressing nursing facility with people who didn't care about their health and wellbeing. That's not the way it has to be and that's not the way it is in Savannah Valley.

The characters in these books celebrate life and retirement in fun and imaginative ways after facing unexpected challenges. Here, new friendships are made, new horizons open, and a lifetime of experience and acquired wealth is celebrated.

Each book in the series is inspired by true events unique to each author. Sit back, relax, and allow yourself to be transported to the glorious and prestigious retirement community known as Savannah Valley.

Love After : Dreams Still Come True
by Russell Gray & Mona Guarino

All About Henry : Rich Widower of Savannah Valley
by Lyle Lee Jenkins

Maestro : Songteller of Savannah Valley
by Rick & Stacie Fessler

Nightingale : Say Goodbye to Yesterday
by Tony Lopes

Rich Widows of Savannah Valley
by Mitzi Perdue

Ruby : Magic Comes From the Heart
by Randall Kenneth Jones

markvictorhansenlibrary.com/savannah-valley

CONTENTS

AUTHOR'S NOTE

Now in our sixties, we're old enough to realize how the world has changed since we were young. Men are less stoic. Women are bolder. People are much more open about publicly sharing the details of their lives, opinions, and experiences.

Ironically, both of us are mostly private people. Yet in the wake of losing our spouses, each after four decades of marriage, we've come to appreciate those who've been vulnerable and caring enough to share with the world their valuable experiences and wisdom . . . lessons gleaned from their own painful losses.

We're of the opinion that each person's journey through the process of being widowed, grieving, accepting, adjusting, and ultimately starting an entirely new phase of life after loss is as unique as their individual fingerprint. We've not found any other widows or widowers whose situation, feelings and lessons fully resonated with us individually or as a couple. But each story of loss we've discovered has provided some valuable insight or inspiration . . . another clue as we pushed into our own very uncertain and often uninviting future without the loves of our lives.

So with the encouragement of our friends Mark and Crystal Hansen, we're taking some of the most important lessons from our own journeys into love after loss, and sharing them with you through the fictional lives of Jeff Diamond and Kimberly Langley.

For both privacy and entertainment purposes, Jeff and Kimberly's story is fictional. But the hurts, fears, hopes and joys are drawn right from our own real-life experiences.

Whether you've already suffered loss or someday will . . . our prayer is that *Love After* inspires you to live and love better in your own here and now. And if you ever find yourself despondent and drowning in sorrow after losing an epic love . . . wondering if you could or should love again . . . we hope *Love After* inspires you to explore the possibility with curiosity and wonder.

Neither of us thought we'd ever love again, much less marry, or have anything more than a consolation prize relationship. Yet, despite the fact we both dearly loved our departed spouses, and their memories will always occupy a sacred place in each of our hearts, we've discovered it's both possible and beautiful to *Love After*.

DEDICATION

To our late spouses Cheri Gray and Gene Guarino,
two of the most loving souls God ever created.
You taught us so much about forever love, fidelity, and
faith. You live in our hearts forever.

To our brave and amazing children
ten monuments to the lives and loves we lost.
Your courage, support, and companionship
as we all journey together into a family future
none of us wished for or imagined
is inspiring beyond words.
We love you.

CHAPTER ONE

Kimberly

2015

The phone rang, and Kimberly chided herself for forgetting to silence it. She avoided talking in the car whenever she could. Her preference was to enjoy the quiet and solitude.

Cole, who had been their driver for almost twenty years, was standing by the car, an open umbrella in his hand, as she walked out of her building. "Good afternoon, Mrs. Langley." Kimberly smiled and ducked her head under the umbrella.

"Cole, I'm never going to give up on telling you to please just call me 'Kimberly.' I wish you'd just humor me." He stopped himself before he spoke the words, *of course, Mrs. Langley*, and he gave, "Okay Kimberly," a try instead.

She smiled and slid into the back of the black sedan in her pencil skirt and three-inch Chanel slingbacks. Cole shut the door with a thud, walked to the driver's seat, closed the umbrella, and got in the car. He'd be driving Kimberly from 401 Park Avenue to meet her husband Andrew for a late lunch at Nobu downtown.

For almost two decades Cole had a front seat view to all the goings-on of the Langley's' lives, especially that of Kimberly Langley. She was always kind, always composed. She always said the right things as he drove her to and from one event to another. When an evening was over, she often slid

into the car, sighed with relief, kicked off her shoes, and told Cole how she couldn't wait to be home. "Home" was a five-story pinnacle penthouse on Park Avenue with over 9,000 square feet of space and a private terrace the size of a small bedroom. The walls and walls of windows let in showers of light, and the interior featured 24-foot ceilings and a private elevator. And that was just one of the Langley residences.

Cole adjusted the rear-view mirror when he caught a glimpse of Kimberly's face. It wasn't the first time he noticed this expression. There was a look in her eyes that told him her mind was wandering—she was somewhere far, far away.

Cole was right. Kimberly was lost in thought. She had just returned from a weekend in Savannah Valley with her friend Cheryl Piedmont. She couldn't stop reliving the magic of those three days. Time with Cheryl always left her feeling revived. Cheryl was her dearest friend, they'd been incredibly close since college, and she admired Cheryl more than almost anyone she knew. Cheryl was courageous and in constant pursuit of "living authentically." Cheryl's most recent transformation transpired when she divorced her husband and followed her passion for teaching yoga. Women over fifty flocked to her classes, which she branded as Warrior Woman classes.

"If you are lucky to have your health at our age," Cheryl said during Kimberly's visit, "then you have all that wisdom to live your best life." While Cheryl's words inspired Kimberly, it was the serenity she found during her brief visit to Savannah Valley that left the biggest impact.

Cole turned left down Lexington, and Kimberly leaned

back in the car. These quiet moments were often rare. In her forty years of marriage to Andrew Langley, something or somebody was always interrupting every opportunity she had to just sit in silence and breathe. As Cole navigated the hustle of the constant city traffic, Kimberly could not stop thinking about Savannah Valley. Sure, the Valley was striking in its opulence and memorable for its five-star amenities, but Kimberly was no stranger to luxury. There was something deeper than the materialism which had in these years defined the core of Kimberly's whole life. For reasons she couldn't quite explain, Savannah Valley reminded her of who she once was. Cheryl would say that Savannah Valley had a way of opening her heart, and Kimberly didn't yet know how much she needed that.

Sheets of rain covered the windshield, and Cole switched the wipers on high speed. From the window, Kimberly watched a mother with two young children scurry on the sidewalk to find cover. The rain reminded Kimberly of the day Andrew proposed. They were on Madison Avenue in the midst of a terrible winter storm—later they'd learned it was reported as the worst Nor'easter recorded in years. But the whipping rain and wind, the traffic lights threatening to snap off their wires overhead—none of it stopped Andrew form kneeling on the sidewalk and presenting Kimberly with a perfect four-carat Tiffany diamond. Of course, she said yes. How could she not?

She was young when they met, and Andrew's persistence was part of his charm. So was his knack for success. He always rode the fast track, determined to follow his vision from the youngest to make partner at a top New York City law firm to his vision to build his own company Heritage Inc. The year Andrew turned forty-five, Heritage Inc. was considered one of the most successful real estate agencies in the world. It was also the year that Kimberly stepped away from her own professional pursuits and devoted her time to being a wife and a mother to their daughter, Jocelyn.

At a recent social function, someone asked Kimberly how long she and Andrew had been married. When she heard herself say forty years, the reality took her breath away. Forty years. Where did all those years of her life go?

The phone, still unsilenced, snapped her out of a trance. Kimberly dug through her purse and after the third ring she answered.

"Hello?"

"Kimberly? It's Steven." The pounding rain on the roof of the car made it hard to hear the voice on the other end of the line.

"Steven?" She leaned forward and plugged her other ear, hoping to hear him better.

Why would Steven be calling her? She checked the time. It was almost one in the afternoon. Andrew and Steven had met for breakfast, she knew. Steven was one of Andrew's partners in a new film project. Andrew, among other things, had recently acquired a new taste for producing. She pressed her ear firmly into the phone.

Steven sounded out of breath. She heard him say Andrew's name. She heard him say hospital.

"We were at breakfast when he suddenly started clutching at his chest. The ambulance came. It all happened so fast. I'm so sorry. Kimberly, are you there?"

Outside the city sped by. Cole braked hard enough to send her lurching back with force. Cars honked.

"Kimberly, can you hear me?"

She could hear him. She heard every word. But there was a part of her that thought if she didn't move a muscle, if she didn't say anything that it could save her from hearing what she suddenly knew Steven would say.

"Kimberly, I am so sorry. It was a heart attack they said. There was nothing they could do. He died in the ambulance on the way to the hospital. I am so, so sorry."

CHAPTER TWO

Jeff

2014

eff Diamond was at home when Jennifer took her last breath. It was exactly what his wife of thirty-nine years had wanted. It was what she requested after the third clinical trial failed.

"I want to go home," she'd said.

They had been in the oncologist's office on the seventh floor, receiving more bad news. Jeff knew what she meant. It was her dying wish, and it was the one thing in the world he didn't want to give her. She looked at him, her eyes translucent, and he could just about make out the face of the young woman he saw for the first time more than forty years earlier.

Jeff and Jennifer met through mutual friends. At the time, he had just graduated Yale and deferred his MBA at Penn to travel to Nepal, where he planned to climb Mount Everest. It had been a dream of his since high school. He'd seen a National Geographic documentary about a man who reached the top but on the descent was almost killed by a near-fatal encounter with a rogue storm. The image of this man holding onto the side of a mountain as ice and snow threatened his lifesaving grip had imprinted itself in Jeff's mind. He wouldn't have classified himself as an adrenaline junkie. His fascination was fueled by a curiosity to understand what it takes for a human being to overcome egregious odds.

Aside from a high school football knee injury, Jeff's own life of privilege had hardly been touched by adversity. The only child of self-made millionaires, he was born into the kind of affluence most people only read about during their morning coffee or on their commute to work. Jeff's lifelong quest to seek adventure was part of a growing philosophy that with hardship comes edge. And, since his destiny was to take the helm of his family's 100-year-old hotel chain, he sought some form of risk as a means to prepare himself for the unexpected. While he grew up in a wealthy household, he never took his life for granted. He was never reckless. But he was afraid of becoming complacent.

Jennifer Harrison, on the other hand, was an academic. Her pursuit of a PhD in art history had been thwarted by her love-at-first-sight encounter with Jeff. On their first date, she became entranced by the way his eyes brightened when he spoke about preparing for his climb. She had never met anyone filled with such passion when they spoke. That spark led her all the way to Nepal with Jeff. She didn't climb, but she stayed at base camp, eagerly awaiting news of his progress each day.

Jeff was so impressed with her loyalty, a quality he found incredibly invaluable. After the trip, he asked her to join him at Penn the next year, where she could revisit pursuing her PhD. Instead of accepting her early admission to the graduate program, however, she found herself pregnant with their son Alexander. While it hadn't been the original plan, she was more than content to stay home and relish her time as a new

mother and wife. After grad school, Jeff's professional life cat-apulted the young Diamond family from wealthy intellectuals to near royalty. Jeff's father, Jeffery Richard Diamond, Sr., had passed away at the age of seventy-five. As the only child, Jeff, by then himself a new father, quieted his drive to seek out adventure, bought a house in the city and another in Litch-field County, put on a suit and tie, and led the family business from being a global hotel chain to becoming an empire. Jeff and Jennifer lived full-time in New York.

They were married forty-two years, and most of it, Jeff would say, was happy—busy, but happy. Neither had taken the time to slow down and notice what was changing between them. It was only when life delivered the shock of her illness that they stopped running in different directions and realized what they had been squandering for years. Then, they began appreciating the time they shared together in earnest.

* * *

Jeff pressed the button of the elevator on the seventh floor of Sloan Kettering Memorial Hospital as Jennifer leaned her body into him. They had found themselves waiting at this same elevator bay many times before, every time holding a different degree of hope. Jeff was a man who spent most of his life chasing adversity and still coming out on top; hope was not something he would settle for. But that day their hopes were shattered irreparably as he held his wife and walked with her into the elevator and rode to the ground floor. They drove to their five-bedroom apartment on Central Park West. He knew that any hope she would survive into the coming year

was long gone. Jeff Diamond could buy just about anything in the world he wanted, but he could not buy himself more time with his wife.

Jennifer died in Jeff's arms. Her favorite flowers, yellow tulips and stargazer lilies, were arranged in vases covering every available surface of the bedroom. With a soft knock at the door, the nurse came in to check her pulse. Aside from the quiet drone and intermittent beeping of machines tracking Jennifer's every breath and the faint rhythm of her heartbeat, the room had been filled with an intense quiet. The nurse clicked a knob overhead, adjusted a wire, and Jeff knew by the look on her face that this was it. He held Jennifer for the last time, whispered, "I love you," and kissed her goodbye. When he was ready, he walked out of their bedroom.

* * *

In the days after Jennifer's death, Jeff found it near impossible to be at home. He couldn't wrap his mind around how quickly all of his perspectives seemed to have changed. All the things Jeff once valued as the markers of happiness were suddenly meaningless. The house no longer felt like a container of joy and comfort as it had over the years—through celebrations, Alex's growth from baby to toddler to child to teen to adult, all the daily routines that defined the rhythm of a life shared together. Now the house was only a stark reminder of Jeff's very new and very real loneliness.

He poured himself the last of the Scotch and stood in the kitchen for a long time. When you are young and raising a family and following your ambitions, you tend not to put

"nurture your relationship" very high on the list. You always think there will be more time. You live as if tomorrow is a guarantee, and not a gift.

He held his glass up in one hand. "I am sorry. I could have been better." The ice cubes clinked in the glass as he took a sip. His eyes blurred with tears. The liquid stung the back of his throat as he finished the drink in one gulp. He walked out of the kitchen and headed to his office.

When he turned on the light, framed pictures of his life over the past forty years stared back at him. Their wedding photo at the Essex House, Jennifer sitting on his lap feeding him a forkful of cake. They looked so young, so ready to take life on. There was a photo of Jennifer and Alex horseback riding on the beach in Bermuda, both of them laughing and smiling and filled with joy. Suddenly, all Jeff wanted to do was sweep all the photos from the table and smash them onto the wood floor.

A leather-bound journal lay on the desk. It had been a gift from his friend Pete Coolidge, Jeff's former co-worker and weekly tennis opponent. Pete had left the city and moved to Savannah Valley a decade ago, but the two kept in touch. Pete had lost his wife many years earlier and had been an especially valuable source of support in recent years when Jennifer had been diagnosed and her health had continued to deteriorate.

Jeff had never journaled before. He opened the book. On the inside was a note from Pete.

I can't say life will ever feel like it once was. But when you can't bear the grief, sit down with a pen and

try writing it all down. This was one thing that saved me. I hope it can do the same for you.

Your friend, Pete

Jeff stood over his desk and leafed through the journal's blank pages. He sat down in the chair and let loose a long breath. He hadn't realized how tired he was, how long it had been since he'd gotten off his feet. He sat for a long time staring at the pages in front of him. Then, for reasons he could not explain, he was overcome with urgency—he needed to write. It wasn't about whether he wanted to or not. He had no choice but to pick up the pen, open the journal, and begin to write.

She's gone.

I knew this day was coming. But I could never have imagined how painful this would feel. I feel like I am drowning. I feel like a stranger in a strange land. What do I do now? What is the next year—next day—hell, the next moment going to look like? Sometimes I think that Jennifer is the luckier one. She is at peace now, and I am the one who has to wake up tomorrow and feel this all over again—and all the days after that. How do I go on with a heart this broken? All the best days of my life are behind me. What is there to look forward to anymore?

CHAPTER THREE

Kimberly

2015

*K*imberly had been on her way to meet Andrew for their two o'clock lunch date when Steven called.

"He didn't make it," Steven said.

Those words bounced and repeated throughout Kimberly's brain nonstop as the following seconds, minutes, hours, and days unfolded before her.

The day of Andrew's death was a complete blur. Someone must have called Jocelyn because she arrived at the hospital. Kimberly was in a waiting room. There was a clock on the wall. People came in and out. A counselor came in. A doctor came in. There were heartfelt apologies, looks of sympathy. There were Andrew's belongings in a plastic bag handed to her. His watch. His wallet. His wedding band. She had no memory of how she got home. She suddenly found herself there, aware in an excruciating way with how different everything suddenly felt. Her life was now—and always would be—defined by a distinct "before" and an "after."

No amount of sleep. No amount of vodka. No amount of time in bed binge-watching ridiculous shows one after another. None of it soothed her, but it did provide moments of relief. But when she awoke again or when the buzz wore off or when the TV annoyingly asked if she wanted to "still continue watching"—she remembered she was still living in the after. She relived the pain of losing Andrew all over again. Before, she had been Andrew Langley's wife. Before she had a life defined by that role. And even as she wished with her whole heart that she had been more attentive, less critical throughout their marriage, in this aftermath, she realized just how much she could not imagine a life or a future without him.

She played back in her head the last morning they woke up together. He had gotten up before her, per the usual. She heard him on the phone while she was still in bed. He took a shower then turned the television on low to listen to the news. He buttoned the cuffs of his shirt. She could not recall his last words to her. He kissed her goodbye. They were both holding their phones. She tried to remember if there were signs. Did he have any idea that as he grabbed his keys, smiled, and said, "See you later," that he was going out that door for the very last time?

People called relentlessly. Kimberly could tell by their soft voices, their long pauses, their questions about food or dropping by, they had no idea what to say or how to help. She turned them all away. She hated feeling like a burden. She hated feeling needful. With a wave of her hand, she said she was okay, she didn't need anything, she was just fine. But that couldn't have been farther from the truth.

Days after the funeral and people had dispersed and resettled into their daily lives, Kimberly was reminded of something her mother had said after her husband, Kimberly's stepfather, had died many years ago.

"Loss is about the little things," she had said. "The way the mail piles up on the counter unopened, or how he always asked for more coffee but left it sitting cold for most of the day. These are the reminders; the things you miss most about the person you shared life with."

Kimberly thought of this as she walked into Andrew's closet and pressed her face against his shirts and ties. She inhaled deeply and closed her eyes. She could still smell him. There, in the privacy of her own bedroom closet, is where she sobbed.

This was not the way things were supposed to happen. At fifty-eight, with more than half of her life come and gone, she could not comprehend the truth that she was now alone.

She called Cheryl.

Cheryl's response was instant. Pack a bag and meet me in Savannah Valley.

At first the notion of leaving seemed impossible. She had a responsibility to be home and be there for her daughter. Not to mention the weight of grief had rendered Kimberly inert. She could hardly muster the energy to make a cup of coffee, how would she find the motivation to travel? Lifting her body out of bed felt like an immense effort.

"Go, Mom," Jocelyn said as soon as she'd learned of Cheryl's offer. Seeing her once-energetic mother so paralyzed, so reticent was unnerving for Jocelyn. The idea of her mother going somewhere and doing something seemed like the best possible option to Jocelyn.

Kimberly had felt like everything was a struggle, even

going for a walk with Jocelyn around the block. Though she thought she was concealing it well, she was under constant pressure to be stronger than she was, to continue shielding her daughter like she had always done.

"This will all be here when you get back," Jocelyn spread her arms wide, gesturing to the house. She walked into the house and opened the drapes and the windows to let some fresh air in.

Kimberly sighed, picked up the phone, and called Cheryl. The arrangements were made, and she would be in Savannah Valley a week or so before Christmas.

"I know it might feel too soon, Kimberly, but the Christmas party here in the Valley is pretty amazing. You can be my date," Cheryl said.

Kimberly smiled for the first time in what felt like weeks. "Well, a party is the last thing on my mind. But..." Kimberly said, recalling her last visit with Cheryl, "Savannah Valley has a way of bringing out the best in me."

CHAPTER FOUR

Jeff

2015

The year caved in. Twelve months blew by, and I cannot recall what I did, where I went, who I talked to. Holidays are like any other day now. Birthdays are brutal. On Jennifer's birthday last week, she would've been sixty. Alex and I went to the movies. I can't even remember what we saw. A comedy, I think. A quarter of the way through the movie, I went to the bathroom, looked in the mirror, and cried. I can't imagine what a stranger would have thought, seeing me, a grown man sobbing in the public bathroom of a movie theater. When I returned to my seat, I could tell Alex was worried. I managed a smile. I want to be strong for him, but most days, I have no idea how I find the strength to get out of bed, to face the hours, to go through the motions of everyday life. Pete keeps asking me to come spend time with him in Savannah Valley. Maybe I should go before Christmas is here. I don't want another winter holiday like last year—that's for sure. It was awful.

***

At night, sometimes for two, three hours at a time, Jeff wrote in his journal. His pen moved across the page as if possessed. His thoughts were an endless stream. He filled page after page with questions, reflections, with the swirl of emotion that left him sobbing most nights. He had no idea where the words were coming from. He had never thought of himself

as a writer. But every time he put his pen to the page, he was transported. He could write the things he was most afraid to say aloud to anyone. In those moments, he felt as close to God as he ever had.

Everything reminded him of Jennifer. When her favorite apples were in season at the grocery store. The wine they used to drink together felt like it was everywhere. The bottles still rested on the kitchen counter unopened. Jeff had long since given up drinking, but he could not bear to get rid of them. Jennifer always asked him to cut back on his drinking, but it wasn't until she was gone that he was actually able to do it. When he reflected on those conversations, he wished he had been kinder, more available. Why hadn't he really listened to what she was asking of him? It was only in her final days that he found a space within himself to love her the way he wished he always had. Why did he wait so long?

The check-ins, calls, and texts from his friends and his son Alex became farther and farther spaced out, moving from daily to weekly to once a month. But the gut punch of his grief stayed persistent, almost constant. The intensity and severity may have lessened slightly, but the feelings were still a strong gust powerful enough to nearly knock him over at times. In those moments, however, now he reached for his journal and a pen.

What is it about life that makes us take for granted what we have? Why do we so easily forget that love and life are not a guarantee? Time can be so strange.

Jennifer has been gone a year, but some nights when I get home, I still expect to find her sitting up in bed with a book in her hands—just like she was for so many years of our marriage. My mind plays tricks on me. In an instant, I can travel back to when my life was intact, to when this pain was nothing I'd ever experienced. Last night, I set a place for her at dinner. I propped up her photo across from me, and I talked to her and told her about my day. I asked her for guidance. I showed her the love and gratitude I never did when she was still here.

Alex sends me old photos when he stumbles across them. He thinks he is helping me. But every time I see an image of our past, I glimpse what can no longer be. It's like someone is pressing a tender bruise. Will it always feel this way?

Pete continues to invite me to Savannah Valley. He thinks getting away will help. He thinks that the space is something I need—to be somewhere new, away from all the reminders. The thought of playing tennis, of walking in the sunshine, of enjoying life for even a second fills me with guilt that wrecks me all over again. How can I let myself enjoy things when she's still gone? Is there even a point to it?

After what felt like the hundredth call from Pete, Jeff finally agreed to get on a plane. He would finally leave the city

and spend time with Pete in Savannah Valley over Christmas. Jeff hadn't traveled since Jennifer's death. In fact, he hadn't been out much at all except when Alex forced him out of the house.

At times, Jeff hardly recognized who he had become. The once charismatic and adventurous spirit, the charming and gregarious parts of him that led to his success had gone dormant. He was an amalgam of grief and despair, and he felt that he was aging faster by the day. When he found the energy to get up, get dressed, and get outside, he paused throughout the process, staring at himself in the mirror, fighting back tears at the unfamiliar face looking back at him. Is this how the rest of his life would be? He searched his reflection for that man he once was—the man who found the motivation to get up and go no matter what. "Was that person gone forever?" he couldn't help but ask himself.

Pete Coolidge knew that Jeff would eventually find his way to Savannah Valley, with or without Pete's encouragement. Before Jennifer became sick, Jeff purchased a property there. The investment made financial sense, and Jeff liked the idea of it as an option for retirement when he and Jennifer were ready. At that point, retirement felt like the far-off distant future. Now, here he was, a retired widower grieving a future he would never have.

He called Alex after he secured a plane.

"Hey, bud. I wanted to let you know you are off the hook this Christmas. I am leaving in two days for Savannah Valley for a bit."

Alex was on his way out the door in a rush when his father had called. When he learned what the call was about, he slowed himself down to talk. "That's a surprise, Dad. But a good surprise, I think. Glad to hear you're ready to get yourself off the sofa a bit, finally."

His son's words stung, but Jeff answered without letting his voice show the pain. "You know what they say, Alex: new year, new you."

Alex checked the time and realized he needed to get out the door. As the last family member still working in the family business, he knew that it was on him to set an example. His father always valued punctuality and reliability—although since his mother died, Alex wasn't sure what his father valued anymore.

"Good for you, Dad. Never too late for new philosophies."

Jeff smiled. "You know me, son," Jeff said, "Always up for an adventure."

"Glad to hear you say that, Dad," Alex said, locking the front door to his new place on Madison just a few blocks from where his father lived.

"I will call you when I land. Maybe you can come visit after Christmas. I'm sure hanging out with a bunch of old widowers is exactly how you want to ring in the new year."

"Dad," Alex rolled his eyes at his father calling himself "old." He never thought of his father as old until recently, and he didn't like it. "Why wouldn't I? After all, it will let me meet the new you, right."

"Right you are," Jeff said. "Merry Christmas. I assume you are skiing over the holiday?"

"You would assume wrong, Dad. Work is crazy right now. My plan is far more mundane. Work and ordering in from Shun Lee is more likely. Maybe watch the game while I catch up on paperwork."

"Work on Christmas? What do you think your mom would have to say about that?"

Jeff wanted to tell his son to forget work. These were the best years of his life. Shouldn't he spend them far away from the corporate life? Work would always be there, but life—real life, the stuff that matters—could pass him by before he knew it if he wasn't careful.

"I think I'm not the only one Mom would have a thing or two to say right now, Dad. I gotta go. My car is here."

After he hung up, Jeff realized how glad he was that he was making this trip—he knew Jennifer would have been glad too.

CHAPTER FIVE

The Arrival, Jeff

On the drive from the airport to the front entrance of the Valley, Jeff found himself looking out the window and admiring the color of the sky. It had been so long since he'd allowed himself to notice anything of beauty. A few months earlier, he likely would have turned away and said, "Who cares about the sunset? My wife is dead." But something in the air here in Georgia felt different. Ever since he got off the plane and the warm breeze brushed his skin, he felt something shift.

Arriving at his Savannah Valley property buoyed his spirits even more. He had only seen pictures sent over from the Heritage Real Estate Agency, so this was the first time seeing the place in person. It was a Frank Lloyd Wright replica, 1920s midcentury modern. The property boasted a surprising abundance of mature trees for such a newly constructed residence. The backyard could have been mistaken for a national forest preserve.

Jeff drove around the circular driveway and parked the car a few feet away from the front entrance. Light bounced from the windshield out toward the horizon and the clouds dipped under the tree line. He sat for a long while, absorbing the slower pace that surrounded him. This was new. He felt Jennifer guiding him to ease up, take a breath. He could

almost hear her voice whisper, "You are going to be okay, Jeff." He turned the engine off, stepped out of the car, lifted his suitcase from the trunk, and walked up the path to his front door.

He had just begun surveying the contents of the house when Pete called.

"Welcome home, old friend."

"Hey, Pete. I have to say, you were right." He leaned against the white marble counter looking around the bright, open space. "It feels nice to be here."

"Yeah? Well, I know two things for certain. First, I am always right. And second, I can't wait to beat your ass on the tennis court. We're reserved for two o'clock. You better start warming up now."

Pete's lightheartedness was like opening a window inside Jeff's chest. It was the first time he felt like someone was talking to him as if his wife hadn't died, as if he were himself again. He watched the trees dancing in the wind in his backyard and wondered if he could be himself again.

"I've gotta say I disagree on both counts, Pete. I'm afraid you're the one who needs to worry about warming up. Believe me, I am ready to play more than you know."

CHAPTER SIX

Kimberly

ime felt like a tide pulling the debris of Kimberly's shock into the depths of an ocean. Cheryl always said a change in location is good for the mind and body, and Kimberly couldn't help but agree. As each day passed, Kimberly found it possible to finally relax— even on the nights when the sadness overcame her. From her bed, she watched the first hint of daylight touch the sky and would sigh with relief, saying to herself, "I survived one more night."

Jocelyn called on Christmas Eve morning. They hadn't spoken since Kimberly arrived in Savannah, both agreeing to give each other a little space and time. Jocelyn wanted her mother to feel free to settle in and take care of herself, and Kimberly wanted to show her daughter that she could do just that. Kimberly planned to stay in Savannah Valley until New Year's, and Jocelyn assured her she would take care of any obligations at home in New York.

Her daughter's voice was an overwhelming comfort after almost ten days of being away.

"How are you doing, Mom?"

Kimberly was on the patio watching a hummingbird flit from one magnolia bush to the other. "Taking it day by day," she said.

Jocelyn laughed. "That didn't take long. You sound like Cheryl."

"Is that a bad thing?"

"Not at all, Mom. It just doesn't sound like you is all—but I like it."

Whether it was Cheryl's influence or just the time away, Jocelyn found immense comfort in how relaxed her mother sounded. She was relieved to know she was faring better even if she was far away.

"How are you doing, darling?" Kimberly asked.

"You know me, Mom. I am soldiering on, just like Dad always said."

Kimberly sighed. "Soldiering on" was a term Andrew had loved to use. Even through the worst of the inevitable conflicts that arose in his business dealings, Andrew's response was always to just "soldier on." Emotional, financial, social—any turmoil that arose, he always focused on getting through.

"I know you are, Jocelyn. But it has to be hard. It's okay not to always be okay."

Her daughter's resistance tightened her voice, "I got it, Mom. I am strong."

"You are strong, Jocelyn. Probably even more than you realize. But you don't always have to be strong—"

"Mom, I called to talk about you, not me. I don't want you to worry about me. I'm fine."

Jocelyn was always uncomfortable talking about feelings, and Kimberly relented to drop it. She knew better than to push her right now. "What do you want for Christmas? I can't believe I'm just now asking. It's almost here!"

Jocelyn replied, "Just send me a photo of you and Cheryl at the gala."

Kimberly smiled. "That's all you want for Christmas this year? A photo of two old ladies?"

"I am not asking for a photo of two old ladies, Mom. I am asking for a photo of you and your best friend."

"You have always known the right things to say."

"Where do you think I got that from?"

Kimberly hung up and exhaled. Ten days in Savannah Valley, and it felt as if she had been there for years. Her pain had not dissolved, and she hadn't expected it to, but being away had diffused the throb of her incessant worry. She accepted this shift in her feelings as if it were its own kind of freedom.

SV

CHAPTER SEVEN

Savannah Valley Family

heryl's house was a sanctuary. Every corner was an invitation for Kimberly to sit down, put up her feet, and relax. Velvet couches and plush rugs, exotic textiles interspersed with minimalist clean lines— her home was a showcase of design but with a comfortable, lived-in feel. When Kimberly was in Cheryl's house, she didn't want to leave, but Cheryl made sure she did.

"You have to move your body," Cheryl insisted, waking Kimberly for an early morning hike. Miles of trails ran the perimeter of the property. A clearing on one path gave way to a wide-open field of sunflowers as tall as trees.

Cheryl and Kimberly arrived there just as the sun began to cast its glow across the field. Kimberly squinted and shadowed her eyes to block the glare. Cheryl put on her sunglasses. Arm-in-arm, they looked out at the sunflowers stretching their thick stems like beanstalks. Kimberly pointed to two trees in the distance, one appeared to be leaning against the other.

Most mornings the women were early enough to have the trails all to themselves. But this day, they heard footsteps and heavy breathing. Cheryl spotted her friend Miriam walking toward them.

Miriam had recently turned seventy, but she looked ten

years younger. Clad in expensive athletic wear, she approached the ladies and took a handkerchief from her fanny pack to wipe the perspiration from her brow.

"You're up early," Cheryl said, opening her arms to hug Miriam.

Watching two grown women share such affection made Kimberly realize how few hugs she had offered—much less received.

Still holding onto to Cheryl's shoulders Miriam pulled away and responded, "You inspired me to wake up early and get this body moving."

Cheryl smiled, clearly overjoyed at this.

"Seriously," Miriam continued, tears glinting in her eyes. "You changed my life, Cheryl."

Kimberly had observed so many women taking time to hug Cheryl and express their gratitude for her help. Whether she'd guided them through stretches and exercises to relieve pain or something as profound as changing a life, it seemed that Cheryl touched a lot of lives in Savannah Valley.

"I didn't do the changing, Miriam. That was all you."

Miriam nodded. "Well, it was me, then, but you and your yoga definitely helped."

Cheryl waved her arms to the field of flowers. "And these plants and flowers, of course. And this fresh air!" She took a deep breath and Miriam put her hands on her heart.

After arriving in Savannah Valley, Miriam had tried yoga for the first time in the hopes of helping her chronic back pain. Reluctantly, she walked into Cheryl's class at the health club,

set her mat up in the back of the room, lay down, and listened to Cheryl's instructions.

"Listen to your breath. Come into your body. Listen to your heart. What is it calling for right now?"

Miriam had never heard anyone talk that way, and she found herself moving her body in ways she had not thought were possible. All the years of tension and stress she had been holding felt like they were pouring out of her.

Cheryl introduced herself to Miriam after class. "How do you feel?"

Miriam paused as she stood. "I feel," it took Miriam a moment to find the word, "...amazing."

Cheryl put her arm around Miriam and said, "Well, good! Because that's the way you deserve to feel."

For Miriam, hearing the word "deserve" was life changing. From then on, she chose to do things that gave her that same amazing feeling—whether it was yoga, hiking, or addressing the stodgy ways her marriage was holding her back from living.

Her partner Doug was set in his ways, and all the nagging and prodding Miriam did wouldn't change his stubbornness. He refused to try yoga. He refused to walk with her. And she refused (up until now) to forgive Doug for cheating on her years and years ago.

From the moment she tried that first yoga class, however, Miriam began living her life according to what she deserved—not what was expected. She committed herself to doing what Cheryl encouraged all the students in her classes to do: live the best life now.

* * *

The three women looked out into the field until Miriam turned to Kimberly. "You must be Kimberly. Cheryl talks about you all the time." Miriam took off her sunglasses and placed them on her head. She stood back to survey the two women. Cheryl and Kimberly were about the same height and aside from the color of their eyes—Cheryl's brown and Kimberly's green—they looked like they could be related.

"You two look like sisters, Miriam said, "Did anyone ever tell you that?"

Cheryl and Kimberly glanced at each other and smiled.

Kimberly answered: "Only ever since college. We've been told we could pass for fraternal twins."

Miriam held out her hand which was sparkling with diamonds. "Well, any friend of Cheryl's is an instant friend of mine."

Before Kimberly took her hand, Cheryl said, "Kimberly is far more than a friend to me. She is family."

"Well, then," Miriam said, spreading her arms wide again, "welcome to the Savannah Valley family, Kimberly."

They said their goodbyes at the edge of Cheryl's road. "See you at the big gala," Miriam called, her voice pitching in excitement. "Before I lived here, I dreaded Christmas. But, now, it's like I'm a kid again, waiting for Santa Claus."

Cheryl nodded. "I used to lie to my ex-husband, claiming a headache to get out of all the Christmas obligations. Now, I order my dress for this celebration a year in advance."

Miriam's eyes widened. "I can't wait to see that number on you!"

Cheryl smiled. "This one will be wearing the best number." She pointed to Kimberly.

"In that case, I'm going to have to keep you away from Douglas," Miriam said, rolling her eyes, the irony dripping in her voice.

Cheryl asked, "Is everything between the two of you okay?"

Miriam thought for a moment. "We are okay—as in he's not going anywhere. It's just that he seems so old, and I feel like I am reborn." She stared off into the distance and then suddenly checked the time." Anyway, this is a much longer conversation. I have to run to the salon. I have an appointment in twenty minutes."

"We will be right behind you." The three women waved goodbye as Miriam took off back to her place, less than a mile away.

When they returned to Cheryl's house, Kimberly took a dip in Cheryl's saltwater infinity pool. Each time she dove into the cool water, it was as if she were washing away another layer of heaviness. She climbed out of the pool and dipped a toe in the nearby hot tub. Just then she spotted Cheryl walking into the meditation room off the flower garden. Cheryl had designed it to replicate an old Tibetan Temple. Kimberly grabbed a robe and walked barefoot across the yard to join Cheryl.

Cheryl's meditation room was a glass and wood structure with floor-to-ceiling windows that reflected light from every side and gleamed like quartz crystal. The interior was empty

except for a few cushions on the polished floor. A small low table with votives sat underneath a framed quote that read, "We are most alive when we are in love."

Kimberly opened the sliding glass door. Cheryl's back was toward her. She was seated on a cushion with her hands on her lap. The sun's rays beamed into the room, beckoning Kimberly to walk inside. After a few minutes, Cheryl turned and patted the floor with her hand signaling for Kimberly to sit down next to her.

One of the many things Kimberly appreciated about Cheryl was no matter how charismatic and free-spirited and wild her friend was, she always held space for the two to sit and just be. In those silences is when Kimberly felt her emotions surge like a wave. Cheryl reached for her hand and told her to just breathe.

"It's just your heart," Cheryl said. As uncomfortable as it was for her, all Kimberly could do was sit there and let the tears stream down her face. She closed her eyes and felt all of Savannah Valley encircle her with comfort, as if the place itself were holding her in its embrace.

* * *

People talk about Savannah Valley as a hub for the rich and the famous. And perhaps that is true. There's the architectural beauty of each home and the plentiful five-star (some say "six-star") amenities—everything from massage therapy to cutting-edge spa treatments. There are flagship designer stores that line the center of town, a shopper's paradise and a destination for the fashion obsessed. The community boasts

nine restaurants, half of which earned Michelin stars, and two award-winning golf courses, the grass court champion tennis club, the new theater attracting some of the best talent in the world. Savannah Valley residents had come to expect services so outstanding it was as if each home came with its own genie in a bottle to grant a new wish every year.

Despite all that, over time what surpassed Savannah Valley's unparalleled luxury was the founders deep respect for the land itself. The original developers, in their mission to attract a high caliber of conscious and compassionate residents, hired a design team that approached construction with a serious consideration to Savannah Valley's natural surroundings. The homes were engineered to preserve precious resources, and phrases like "good energy," "feng shui" and "holistic culture" were the benchmarks of what made Savannah Valley the newest wave of modern retirement luxury living.

People who bought homes in Savannah Valley cared about being good to the Earth, and that made all the difference in the culture the community attracted. Those values poured through every detail—from the materials used to build new structures, to the water filtration system, to the gardens and grounds. That kind of attention to detail and compassion for the world cultivated a feeling of living among people who appreciate their surroundings and never take them for granted.

In Cheryl's meditation room, the two women let their gazes settle out into the distance.

Kimberly broke the silence. "This is all the support I need." She took Cheryl's hand.

She understood Kimberly was responding to Cheryl's suggestion to check out one of the local bereavement support groups. The two had been enjoying dinner at Kimberly's favorite spot; with extra outdoor seating, it was often the quietest of the nine restaurants.

Kimberly had been struggling in the days leading up to the holidays. She felt guilty being away from Jocelyn. She felt guilty for enjoying a good time—even a good meal. Cheryl was careful with her words when she made the suggestion, but Kimberly had still responded defensively. She'd immediately bristled at the phrase "support group."

"Kimberly, it is just a suggestion. There are so many people—"

Before she could finish Kimberly interrupted her. "I know. So many people have told me a support group saved their lives. But..." The tears began to pool in her eyes. "Other people's sadness doesn't make me feel better. I don't want to be reminded of my loss. I just want to be normal again." She put her head in her hands and cried.

Cheryl hadn't pushed. She'd let the tears fall and waited until Kimberly was ready to talk more.

Kimberly finally looked up, her eyes red and swollen. "I am not ready Cheryl. This grief," she put her hands on her throat as if she were choking herself, "won't let me go."

She took a sip of wine, put her glass down, and leaned toward Kimberly. "Maybe, Kimmie, it's the other way around."

Kimberly took a sip of her wine. "I don't understand what you mean."

"Maybe it's not about the grief letting go of you. Maybe you need to let go of the grief—let it change into something else."

CHAPTER EIGHT

Christmas Eve Morning

It was midmorning when Jeff decided to head out for a two-mile jog to clear his head. Texts from friends back in the city, usually sent him in his New Balance sneakers off to the gym, but here in Savannah Valley, he opted for a quick run through the neighborhood. Another holiday season meant a flurry of invitations to parties, to meet up with friends—encouragement to do the one thing Jeff felt zero desire to do: meet someone new.

He turned the corner and running toward him was the couple Jeff recognized from the show Pete dragged him to the other day. Savannah Valley's new theater had become a cherished venue, and Jeff remembered Pete telling him that these two people were responsible for elevating the quality of art in Savannah Valley. Jeff remembered their names just as they stopped to say hello.

Ingrid was an attractive woman whose mane of thick silver hair was tied in a low side ponytail. Her husband, Vince, who seemed more out of breath than his wife, was only too happy to use the excuse of seeing Jeff to stop running. He held out his hand to Ingrid as a signal for Ingrid to wait.

"Ingrid! Vince! Nice to see you two again."

"Jeffery Diamond." Ingrid preferred calling people by their full name.

Now that they'd greeted each other, Jeff couldn't think of anything to say. In this past year, his small talk had moved from rusty to nonexistent.

Ingrid and Vince looked at each other. "It's funny we are running into you. I was just telling Vince I know someone you might like to meet. She's coming over New Year's."

Vince stopped his wife before she went any further. "Darling, what gives you the idea that Jeff has any interest in meeting anyone?"

Ingrid looked at him, her smile slightly dimming. "Nobody wants to grow old alone. Besides, what is the hurt in trying to connect two wonderful, single adults?"

Jeff listened to the conversation, wondering when, or if, either of them would care to ask his opinion on the matter. Before their argument could escalate, he held up his hand. "So sorry. I need to get going before my heart rate goes down. I'm trying to beat last week's time."

Seeing Ingrid's face as he attempted to slip away, Jeff followed up with, "And Ingrid, you can tell me all about this friend of yours at the gala."

As he took off, he heard Ingrid say to Vince, "See? I knew he'd be interested in meeting her."

On his way home, Jeff tried to remember the last Christmas Jennifer had been healthy. As he sprinted past the clubhouse toward his street on Elderberry Lane, he couldn't recall the details. Had they been in New York or Connecticut? Did Alex have a girlfriend then? Was that the year she came to the New Year's party? The holidays had been tough enough when Jennifer was so sick; they were near impossible now that she was gone. Jeff promised Pete, however, that this year he would go to the gala and try to get in the holiday spirit. He would put on a tux, stay through dessert, and do his best to make conversation.

It wasn't just Ingrid and friends back in New York interested in finding Jeff a love interest. The subject had come up the previous week with Pete over lunch.

"The thought of starting all over again." Jeff grimaced. "I can't imagine—the dating, the small talk, the making space to build a new life with someone else. All for what? To be crushed by heartbreak or loss. I can't do it again." He took a sip of his tonic water and shook his head, hoping this would end the conversation.

Pete didn't disagree. His wife Sally had died more than twenty years earlier, and she had been his high school sweetheart. After losing her, he had no desire to open himself up to anyone new. Pete moved to Savannah Valley, cut ties with nearly everyone he had known in his life with Sally. There were too many painful memories. The few friends who did stay in touch with him said that it felt like Pete and Sally both died—his absence was so sudden and complete. And that was fine with Pete. He'd just lost the love of his life. To him, that wasn't that different from death.

He held up his glass of rose and made a toast. "To my widowed friend on Christmas Eve. May the only 'love' you find be on the tennis court."

Jeff laughed. He rose from the table, feeling grateful for Pete.

Pete took the last sip of coffee. "You want me to drop you off?"

Jeff gazed at the sun making its climb overhead, the gentle breeze like an invitation to stay outside a little bit longer. "Nah, what do I look like? An old man who can't get around on his own? I am going to walk it."

"Fair enough," Pete said, grabbing his keys and smiling. "Just try not to fall and break a hip, old man."

* * *

Kimberly sat up in bed with her coffee in hand, thinking of her last Christmas with Andrew. They had been in Aspen. Andrew picked up a nasty cold during their trip, so they decided to forego the black tie at The Little Nell. They opted instead for a small dinner at their condo, just the two of them. They indulged in oysters, champagne, and chocolate ganache. She remembered the meal more than she remember things they had said to one another. They'd toasted one another across the long table, mutual wishes for a happy holiday. It all seemed so . . . tiresome. Without Jocelyn there to break the silence, the small gap between them had grown into what felt like a chasm. After so many years, they'd become so used to each other that each might as well have been another piece of furniture, a piece of décor—just something else that was fixture in the life they'd created. When had they stopped really seeing one another? Kimberly hadn't even realized it happened until Andrew was no longer there.

She heard Cheryl on the phone downstairs in full Christmas party mode. Kimberly witnessed Cheryl's home and the

surrounding neighborhoods of Savannah Valley come alive with a celebratory vibe as the holiday approached. Christmas spirit at its finest shone through every light, every special ornament, every little festive detail.

Kimberly smelled the fresh pine from Cheryl's magnificent tree as she walked down the circular stairwell toward the kitchen. The two had spent hours stringing the tree with tiny white lights. Cheryl appointed Kimberly as the one to place the bright silver and gold star on top, as if the task would grant her some unexpected wish. Each ornament had a story, and as Cheryl pulled each relic out of a box, she shared its origin. Most were procured during her travels through India and Asia, and as she hung each one, Kimberly relished hearing her friend share stories of her journeys.

* * *

The day of the gala, Cheryl booked them appointments at the salon with top stylists. She'd arranged for her makeup artist to meet them at the house after lunch. Kimberly knew how much Cheryl looked forward to the Christmas gala, and as much as she wanted to join in the reverie, she couldn't help but feel exhausted at the prospect. Sleep at Savannah Valley was better than it had been back in New York, but she still struggled to feel truly rested. Kimberly caught her reflection in the mirror on her way to the kitchen and stopped to study her face, her ruddy cheeks and puffy eyes.

"I look so tired," she said aloud, uncertain if Cheryl was within earshot.

"Nothing a little makeup and Christmas spirit can't fix,"

Cheryl sang out, handing Kimberly a cup of cinnamon herbal tea.

They looked at one another's reflections in the large wall mirror, and Cheryl, using her best motivational voice, said, "For one night, Kimmie, let yourself feel some joy. That red Valentino hanging in the closet has your name on it. How can you feel anything but gorgeous in that? It was always my good luck dress."

Kimberly looked at her reflection one more time and let Cheryl's words seep into her system. She agreed that perhaps for one night she could let herself enjoy, play dress up, and pretend she was a different woman living an entirely new life. After all, it was just one night.

CHAPTER NINE

A Christmas Romance

there had been much discussion about the dress code and theme for the Christmas gala in Savannah Valley. There was talk of turning it into a masquerade ball or an all-white affair. There were a few pushes to go semiformal, allowing suits and ties in lieu of tuxedos. In the end, the call was made, and nobody was surprised: the black-tie requirement remained. It was hard to change tradition. A new theme however emerged from the founding committee. This year they chose to call the gala a "Christmas Romance" and the decor was planned accordingly. There were even heart-shaped Swarovski crystal napkin holders.

The towering Sky restaurant, the highest point in Savannah Valley with the most jaw-dropping views, was reserved for the gala. In years past, guests had stood with champagne flutes and pointed from the wraparound windows to the decorated houses below. The splendor of the entire Valley was as much on display on Christmas Eve as the fashion trends the women waited all year to showcase for one another.

A glass elevator to the top floor opened to Sky. The already dazzling interior of the restaurant, prized for its globally recognized design, was for one night transformed into a theatrical Christmas masterpiece. Every year the gala promised to

be a "once in a lifetime" spectacle, and every year it fulfilled its promise.

At the entrance to the grand ballroom this year guests were greeted with a tree that rivaled Rockefeller Center. The majestic pine strung with a thousand tiny pave diamonds was nicknamed "starry night" and the pave diamonds were rumored to be genuine.

The tables were decorated as if they were characters in a winter wonderland. Gold-plated China was set upon white organza tablecloths; oversized silk bows were tied onto the backs of each banquet chair. The room looked like a magical scene from a sophisticated fairy tale. There was mystique, without the darkness. White lilies and red roses sprung from Baccarat crystal vases; and the room was flooded with the fragrance of pine and bathed in the amber glow of candlelight. A fifteen-piece band played a jazzy rendition of "Silver Bells," as servers stood at attention in white coats and tails, peeking their heads to catch a glimpse of the guests as they arrived. Jensen, the head maître d', performed a final walk of the room, ensuring not a fork, knife, or spoon was crooked or, worse, missing.

Fashion was theater, and Savannah Valley's guests entered as if they were walking the famed Hollywood red carpet. Jensen took his place at the front of the house to welcome each guest—most he knew by name.

Miriam walked out of the elevator with her partner Douglas Canton. The two had lived together for more than forty years. Rumors swirled, however, that both had been unfaithful

on and off throughout the years, the pair always coming back together when an affair fell apart. Doug, at seventy-five, looked every bit his age as he shuffled in his tuxedo to the entrance of the party. On the other hand, Miriam, thanks to her new passion for Cheryl's yoga classes, could pass for fifty-five on a good night. And this was one of those nights.

"Merry Christmas, Douglas," Pete Coolidge called out, having arrived alone and spotting the couple. Jeff was only a few minutes behind him, having chosen to walk the half mile to the Tower rather than ride with Pete.

Doug turned to shake Pete's hand. "Merry Christmas is right," Doug said. "You can't help but fall under the holiday spirit spell with a venue like this." He turned his head to face the room.

Pete nodded. "Every year they outdo the last." He turned to Miriam, who was radiant in Vera Wang. "Ah, this must be your younger sister."

Miriam's laugh was a bit forced. She'd heard it before, and so had Doug. While she adored the compliment, she knew it made him uncomfortable, and when he was uncomfortable, she knew he'd spend most of the night at the bar—and definitely not with her on the dance floor.

Pete grazed Miriam with a peck on the cheek. She smelled of light musk and rose. "Didn't mean to insult you, Doug. Why don't you get your revenge on the tennis court next week?"

Doug smiled tightly. "I think I would rather challenge you to a duel at the bar."

* * *

The air was unusually warm and stagnant for December in Savannah Valley. A third of the way to the Gala, and Jeff started to perspire. He stopped just as the moon gleamed in its fullest potential overhead. A sudden breeze swept through, and he welcomed the moment to cool off. With his eyes closed he breathed in the night air and felt compelled to talk to Jennifer. He ached for her presence.

"I am trying," he said aloud. "I am trying to figure out how to make a life without you."

When he opened his eyes again, he looked down and noticed something shimmering on the ground at his feet. He knelt to get a closer look and saw that it was a stone—nearly polished to a gleaming finish, making it appear like marble. He picked up the stone and held it under the moonlight, and when he turned it around to inspect it, he noticed a heart etched into its center.

There was a time in his life when Jeff would have laughed at the idea of things like "signs." Jeff's pragmatism, a quality that made him successful in business, did not lend itself to metaphysical beliefs or new age ideologies. Yet, standing with that stone in his hand and feeling the gentle breeze that seemed to have arisen out of nowhere, a new belief started to emerge: Maybe Jennifer was here with him. He was as certain of that as he was of the stone in his hand.

She was not there in the form he had ached for all these months, but she was there in a different way. Memories of their life flashed through his mind, and the grief that sat in his heart like a weight pulling him down started to lift. The

sadness those memories used to engender softened into something a little more joyful. He realized he was feeling grief again, but this time it was shaded with something even more powerful—love.

Let me go. Let me go so that you can love again.

Had anybody asked, Jeff would have sworn in that moment it was his wife's voice whispering in his ear.

Let go and live.

Perhaps there was a time he would have dismissed the whole experience as a delusion. But that night, as he continued his walk toward the Tower, he slipped the stone in his pocket and felt for the first time that he would never truly be alone again.

CHAPTER TEN

It had begun subtle enough. A moment of beauty and grace. Something so perfect and awe-inspiring in its simplicity. But over the years, the sunsets in Savannah Valley had become more than a daily occurrence. They'd become a cherished event—a living watercolor of enchantment and wonder to be appreciated and revered. Residents emerged from their homes just as the temperature dropped a few degrees, and with bottles of champagne in one hand and elaborate picnic baskets in another, they walked together to the green fields next to the clubhouse. There, they would spread blankets and wait in hushed silence for the sky to begin its technicolor dance. The sound of a few cameras snapping shots and the chorus of oohs and aahs would eventually break the quiet, as nature's theater began. The watchers aimed their gaze at the horizon and waited transfixed, not wanting to might miss the moment they all waited for—the inevitable moment when it would seem the sky could not get anymore mesmerizing, and then it did. As the last of the golden rays dissolved into nothingness, the crowd stood in awe, absorbing the beauty of life and the natural world as if they were discovering it for the first time all over again.

That was how it was when Jeff met Kimberly.

CHAPTER ELEVEN

heryl entered the tower in a bespoke white beaded strapless gown. Kimberly was close behind handing the keys to the valet to park Cheryl's hybrid Range Rover. Cheryl strutted through the grand hallway to the elevator with a hand on her hip and her red lips in the perfect pucker of a Hollywood starlet. She was radiant and youthful and, inexplicably, becoming more so with each passing year.

Kimberly was equally show stopping in Cheryl's cherry red Valentino chiffon dress. As she opened the door to enter the Tower, a breeze caught the edge of the fabric, and the dress appeared to dance around her.

"That's what this dress is known for," Cheryl had told Kimberly about this particular chiffon, holding the dress for Kimberly to get a better view of the gown on the hanger. "It's like wearing breath."

Kimberly's blond hair was loose and wavy, just as Cheryl suggested to the stylist. "Why pull that beach wave up and hide what most people pay a lot of money for?"

"Wait a minute," Cheryl added, "I guess I'm 'people.' I pay a lot of money for exactly that." She had thrown her head back and laughed.

As Kimberly tried to keep up with Cheryl's pace, the strap of her shoe loosened, making her nearly lose her balance.

"Damn these heels," she muttered, attempting to right herself on the three-inch Jimmy Choo stilettos Cheryl had encouraged her to wear.

Jeff spotted the two ladies approaching the elevator and held the doors for them. Before she stepped inside, Kimberly bent down to adjust the strap of her shoe. As she stood and walked across the threshold into the elevator, their eyes met, and each of them jolted. Something was awakened deep inside them both.

Kimberly's face grew hot, and she told herself it was from the champagne she and Cheryl had enjoyed before leaving the house. But a part of her knew it wasn't the champagne.

As the elevator doors closed and the glass dome ascended at a faster speed than expected, Jeff stumbled a bit, calling out, "Hold on!" He instinctively grabbed Kimberly's hand. The touch reverberated through every cell in his body, and for a few seconds, he couldn't move or speak.

Their fingers interlaced, and Kimberly became awash in familiarity and comfort, as if she were holding the hand of a dear friend.

As the elevator reached its destination, both Kimberly and Jeff struggled to piece together what had just happened. But their interaction went completely unnoticed by Cheryl. She raced out of the elevator like a kid angling for the front of the line. She couldn't wait to see the Savannah Valley design team's interpretation of a Christmas Romance. She reached back to pull Kimberly along with her, but to her surprise, Kimberly waved her to go ahead.

"I will be right there," she said, putting her hands on her cheeks. "I need a little breath."

Cheryl finally seemed to notice Jeff. She looked back at Kimberly and smiled. "Take all the breaths you need, Kimmie." She raised an eyebrow at Jeff and sauntered off, waving to Jensen and some friends she recognized up ahead.

Jeff and Kimberly stood close to one another, the chemistry in their bodies producing an unexplainable impulse to stay close to each other. Like a magnet pulling them toward one another, neither seemed to be able to turn away. They turned to face each other.

"Have we met before?" Kimberly asked, looking into his eyes, searching for the source of the familiarity she felt.

The room swelled with more arrivals, shrieks of delight, and the low hum of social chatter. But all Kimberly noticed was this man in front of her. Just as she started to lose herself in his gaze, her ever-present grief surfaced once again. She broke the stare and looked at the floor.

Jeff regained his composure and managed to muster his old charms. "You think that line is going to work on me?" He stood back as if to give her a better look. "I mean, I haven't been this trim since college."

She felt an immediate ease and almost laughed as she looked up again. "No, I mean it," she said, crossing one foot in front of the other. "I swear we have met before."

Jeff studied her face. Just as he traced the angle from her neckline to the warmth of her smile, it came to him. "You're Andrew Langley's wife?"

Hearing his name made Kimberly's stomach seize. She felt the color drain from her face.

"We have met before," Jeff confirmed. "At his memorial service at St John's Church. I shook your hand and introduced myself during the reception line."

Kimberly tried to recall the reception line at Andrew's memorial service. She'd leaned on Jocelyn almost the entire day, afraid her own legs wouldn't hold her up. She didn't remember meeting Jeff, but she hardly remembered anything about that day.

"I knew your husband." His eyes softened. "He's the reason I'm here."

"What?" Kimberly suddenly felt like New York, her former life, had followed her here.

"I bought a house here in Savannah Valley through Heritage."

Kimberly took his words in but still they did not register. "Forgive me, but I don't think that's it. I think I'd remember if that's when we met."

Jeff tried to think of when they may have met before but came up blank. Grief had a way of blurring the edges of memory. It was hard to tell sometimes what was real anymore.

But as he listened to Kimberly and watched how her eyes moved when she spoke, he was sure he did know her. He knew her in a way he couldn't recall knowing someone else—ever. They shared something. He could feel it in his gut. Even more, he found himself wanting to protect her, to reach for her, to

hold her, but he shook off the feelings. She was a stranger. He was thinking crazy thoughts.

It was then when she remembered. "It was at a charity event in Soho! We were dance partners briefly!"

Jeff's eyes widened. The only charity event he could remember in Soho had been a few years earlier. He'd only attended because Jennifer had insisted. "The fundraiser for the New York City Arts Foundation?"

"Yes! I was there with my daughter Jocelyn because my husband . . . Andrew . . . was away on business." She heard herself saying Andrew's name and wondered if it was the first time she'd done so since he died.

He smiled as the memory washed over him. "That was definitely Jennifer's event. That was all her."

"I knew your wife. Jennifer, Jennifer Diamond. We met a few times at charity events at the Guggenheim. Her knowledge of art was incredible. She was amazing."

Jeff's smile widened. "That she was." And just like that, he felt the pang of familiar sadness. His instinct was to excuse himself from the conversation, escape the moment and the feelings that were rising within him. Instead, he put his hand in his pocket and squeezed the heart stone between his fingers. He looked to Kimberly and empathized with the longing he could see in her eyes. He'd lost Jennifer more than a year earlier. Kimberly's loss was still so fresh and new. She was at the beginning.

"I am so sorry about Andrew," he said. "It was such a shock."

Kimberly teared up and marveled at her desire to reply, to continue this conversation in spite of her tears. She hadn't let herself appear like this to anyone else but Cheryl. Knowing he knew what she was feeling helped. They shared more than just social circles; they were bonded in shared grief. Eventually, she simply said, "Thank you," and nodded her head.

Jeff resisted his urge to say more. He suddenly felt as if he wanted to tell her so many things, to prepare her for the months ahead of her, to help her navigate the loss. Instead, he turned his head toward the ball room, looked back at Kimberly, and said, "Shall we go inside?"

Kimberly smiled and took a few steps ahead of him toward the entrance. "That's what we are here for."

* * *

The lighting was low enough so nobody could tell who they were as they walked in together, but Kimberly's heart was still racing. She talked herself out of this absurd schoolgirl behavior, telling herself she was making this all up in her head.

Jeff, on the other hand, could not care less who saw them walk into the room together. He was smitten and felt an undeniable responsibility to take care of Kimberly. Jensen greeted them at the entrance. "Merry Christmas to you, Mr. Diamond." Jeff shook Jensen's hand.

"And, hello, Ms. Langley. Ms. Piedmont advised us of your impending arrival. Let me take you to your table."

As fate would have it, Pete was sitting next to Cheryl and signaling to Jeff as the two followed Jensen across the

ballroom to their seats. Miriam and Doug were there, along with Ingrid and Vince. The couples held up their glasses.

"Looks like we got the best table in the house," Ingrid said clinking glasses with Vince.

When the horns blared the last note and the guests cheered, Cheryl turned toward Kimberly and patted the seat next to hers.

"Did you get enough breathing time?" Cheryl winked. She held her hand out to Jeff. "I don't think we have met before. I know I have seen you at the tennis club. But I don't think our paths have crossed. I'm Cheryl Piedmont."

Jeff took her hand and just as voices quieted down, he leaned over to introduce himself. "Jeff Diamond. It is a pleasure to meet you, Cheryl."

"Not as pleasurable as it was to meet Kimmie it seems." She smiled innocently and turned to Kimberly who sat down and reached for her glass to take a sip of wine.

Jeff smiled and turned his gaze toward the place setting in front of him.

"Actually," Kimberly said as servers milled around to fill wine and water glasses, "Jeff and I knew each other already." She gave a pointed glance to Cheryl and stood to introduce herself to Pete. "I'm Kimberly, Kimberly Langley." She stretched out a hand.

Pete leaned in to take her hand and looked at Jeff. "Pleasure, Kimberly. What brings you to Savannah Valley?"

Kimberly smiled at Cheryl. For a brief second, she made eye contact with Jeff. "What brings anyone to Savannah Valley?"

Cheryl raised her champagne flute. "Good question. What brings us here, everyone?" And the eight tablemates held their glasses in the air, as Cheryl made the toast, "Here's to living your best life."

* * *

As the last of the dessert plates were cleared, Kimberly and Jeff found themselves standing together again, this time by the windows gazing at the view. "It's pretty magical here," Kimberly said.

Jeff nodded. "Pete kept telling me to come. It took me a long time to follow through. I don't think he ever would have relented."

Kimberly was amazed at how comfortable she felt talking to Jeff. It was so easy to open up to him.

"I know the feeling. Cheryl would not take no for an answer."

She told Jeff about her previous trip to Savannah Valley to visit Cheryl, how she had dreamed of returning and staying longer. And then Andrew died and . . . travel had felt impossible.

"Life unfolds in ways we never expected, doesn't it?" Jeff said, his eyes shifted downward to the streets below. Cars were pulling to the front and guests were already making their way back to their homes. Unexpectedly, an ache bloomed in his chest. "The nights are the hardest," he said. "Nothing could have prepared me for what those are like."

Kimberly shifted her focus from the window to Jeff's

profile. She nodded. "The worst," she said softly and closed her eyes.

The band announced it was their last set, and Cheryl came to check in with Kimberly, but the pair had no desire to say goodnight.

Pete came over and shook his friend's hand. "Don't forget we scheduled an early game tomorrow."

Jeff smiled. "Even with no sleep, I could still beat you in straight sets with my eyes closed."

Pete laughed. "I will remind you of that tomorrow. Merry Christmas, friend. I am glad you are here."

"Thanks, Pete. You, too."

Kimberly and Cheryl hugged, and Cheryl said she would wait downstairs in the car. Kimberly nodded and assured her she wouldn't be much longer. She turned back to say good night to Jeff but found it hard to say the words.

"Well, Jeff Diamond, thank you for nearly saving my life in the elevator earlier. I don't know what I would have done if you weren't there in my moment of need."

Jeff laughed. "I am glad I was there to catch you, Kimberly." And then he mustered the courage to say what he had been wanting to say to her all night. "If you need to talk, if you need a friend, if you need anything—any hour—please call me." He took out a folded piece of paper from his pocket where he'd written his phone number and a note that read, *Kimberly, I am here for you.*

CHAPTER TWELVE

After the gala that night, Jeff practically skipped home in the moonlight. As he walked up his driveway to the front door and into his home, a lightness seemed to follow him into the house. His reflected on the evening. His walk. The breeze. The stone. He pulled it from his pocket and placed it on the mantle above the fireplace in the living room. It had been so long since his thoughts weren't filled with anger and guilt and unfathomable sadness. Tonight, with relief, he looked at Jennifer's photo on the bookshelf and felt nothing but love and appreciation. Before he could stop himself, he spoke aloud into the darkness, "Thank you."

Thoughts of Kimberly washed over him. He conjured memories of the first time they met, at the dance studio. He had been a different man back then. The fact that they knew each other's late spouses, the fact that their own lives had come together and dispersed and then come together again—this he began to refer to as the great design.

Kimberly was beautiful and Jeff certainly felt a physical attraction to her. But knowing how recently she'd lost her husband; he kept their relationship firmly in the friendship category. And that almost made it feel deeper—and it definitely felt safer. He knew what he needed to do. He reached for a pen and his journal.

What a mystery life is.

Last year I was cursing God. I was fighting reality. I came face to face with the truth that I had no control over my life. None. But tonight, I heard Jennifer's message. She reached me when I needed it most. The more I cling to the life I once had, the more I am going to suffer. Letting go of that life is the ultimate risk. How can I possibly fall into the unknown, not knowing if I will be okay? How does anyone do that. The stone was a sign. Meeting Kimberly again was another sign. An affirmation. I can see the pain in her heart as if it were my own. I wanted to tell her so many things, to guide her through grief and protect her from pain. I want to fix it for her, but I know that I can't. There isn't anything I can say or do to take away her pain. It is enough to let her know I am here, and I am her friend in grief.

And with that, he put his journal down and lay back on the couch, his tuxedo still on. He closed his eyes and rested his hands on his chest. He followed his breath, steady and soft, and listened to the quiet hum of the late-night silence. For the first time in over a year, as his mind quieted down, he drifted off to sleep and did not wake until he heard the morning bird-song out his window.

***

Cheryl and Kimberly stayed up drinking tea well after midnight. They sat on the floor, still in their dresses and makeup, like two high schoolers recounting the events of a school dance. They shared their impressions and opinions of the venue and

the band, they gossiped about Miriam's provocative moves on the dance floor and Douglas's moody silence cloistered at the bar. Finally, having exhausted all other subjects, Cheryl finally found an opening to turn the conversation to Jeff.

Kimberly hugged her knees to her chest, careful to push away any romantic thoughts and fixate on friendship—pure and simple. Though, there was no denying how her eyes brightened, and her voice became immediately more animated when she spoke of Jeff. With Cheryl, she allowed these hints of bliss as she reflected on this unexpected new friendship.

"You said you knew each other?" Cheryl asked shifting from the floor to the chaise. "Tell me about that."

Her eagerness to talk about this with Cheryl surprised her. Perhaps this conversation was a welcome change from all the nights where she cried herself to sleep, keeping so much buried inside herself.

"His wife was active in the arts community. I met her at Guggenheim luncheons. She was a force—but in a quiet way. I wish I had gotten to know her better. But she was always so welcoming and kind. We were mostly acquaintances, but I considered her a friend. Someone I respected." Kimberly thought about Jeff in that moment and what it must have been like for him to lose her.

"About two years ago, Jennifer invited me to a fundraiser at a ballroom dance studio in Soho. It was so unlike the typical silent auctions and dinners—I really wanted to check out the

event. Andrew had been out of town, so Jocelyn attended with me."

"Was the event fun?" Cheryl asked.

Kimberly frowned. "At first it was awkward." She sat up and gestured with her hands. "In the center of this enormous dance studio, we were separated into two lines facing each other. Men were on one side, and women were on the other. The dance instructor explained the steps one at a time. Then we had to turn to our partner facing us and practice."

"Oh my god. A room full of uptight New York art society being told what to do? So far out of their comfort zone." Cheryl laughed.

"Exactly," Kimberly said. "Most of us didn't know where to put our feet or hands. It was like a middle school dance or something—nobody knew what to do. Jocelyn was next to me, and she wouldn't stop laughing. I kept telling her to be quiet, so I could hear the instructions."

Cheryl laughed and nodded her head. "Of course, always the prized student!"

"The next thing I knew, right in front of me was this tall handsome man I had never seen at any of the charity events before. I didn't know he was Jennifer's husband. I don't think we even really introduced ourselves. We just . . . danced. I remember thinking that he was the best dance partner I had all evening." Kimberly paused as if suspended in memory. "That was it. We danced. I don't think we even said goodbye. I don't think I even made the connection that our spouses

knew each other. I'm sure our paths probably crossed at other events over the years though. How could they have not?"

Cheryl put her tea down. "He seems like a really nice guy, Kimmie. And still handsome..."

Kimberly rolled her eyes. "He is a nice guy, Cheryl—a nice friend. He has been through what I have been through."

Cheryl just smiled. She knew Kimberly well enough to know there was more to this than she was saying. But she also knew her friend well enough to know that inserting her opinion or advice was not going to do any good for anyone.

The two friends lay back and let the silence between them expand. Kimberly closed her eyes. It had been more than a month since she lost Andrew. And, as if on cue, there was that pain again, deep within her, squeezing her from the inside out. Right behind it came thoughts of Jocelyn and the life waiting for her in New York. The life she had escaped from but only for a short time. She was leaving Savannah Valley a few days before New Year's. She hoped she would see Jeff before she left. She allowed her thoughts to drift away from New York and toward Jeff and their new friendship as she closed her eyes and drifted off to sleep.

CHAPTER THIRTEEN

Love Is In the Air

The tennis club was quiet on Christmas morning, and Pete was in the pro shop eyeing a new tennis racquet when Jeff raced in. Pete pointed to his watch. "Twenty minutes late? Should I consider this a forfeit?"

Jeff looked around and aside from a few staff members the club looked empty. "Well, it doesn't look like anyone is waiting in line for a court time. Let's go." He turned back to Pete, who was holding a new racquet in his hand, "Or do you need some time to warm up?"

Pete put the racket down and gestured toward the courts. "After you, old man."

"Age before beauty," Jeff said and held his hand out. "Lead the way."

"The only lead I will be taking is on the court." Pete patted Jeff on the back.

With every step, Jeff's body ached with fatigue. Despite a full night's sleep, he still felt exhausted. "Honestly, I think this time you may be right."

"Late night?" Pete asked grabbing a few tennis balls from the bench nearby.

"Let's just say, it was a night to remember." He walked to the other side of the court, and thoughts of Kimberly wafted through his mind.

As suspected, the match was a battle, and in the end, Jeff succumbed to his first defeat in weeks. Out of breath, he walked over to the net to shake Pete's hand.

"Seems like a Christmas romance has you under its spell," Pete said.

"Yeah," Jeff wiped the sweat from his forehead. "Clearly the spell took away my serve. Consider that win my Christmas gift to you."

"How about I buy you lunch to soothe your pain?"

"If it were just that easy."

The waiter came by as soon as they sat down at the table and handed them menus. Within minutes, Jeff announced he was ready to order. He hadn't eaten much the night before, and he hadn't realized how hungry he was until he sat down. "I will have the special club sandwich and tonic water with ice."

Pete eyed the menu. "The salmon, please, and a glass of rosé."

Tables started to fill around them and just as the waiter left to place the order, Pete spotted Miriam. He waved to her and Miriam, fresh from yoga with Cheryl, walked toward the table, waving and smiling.

"Merry Christmas, gentlemen. Nice to see you both up and moving your bodies."

Pete stood to give Miriam a kiss on the cheek. There was that scent again from the other night, musk and rose.

"I don't mean to be rude," Jeff put his hand on his heart, "but this body can't find the energy to stand up."

Miriam dismissed Jeff's comment with a brush of her hand, "Oh, Jeff, please just be yourself."

Pete sat down again and asked Miriam if she wanted to join them.

She looked around before answering. "I am supposed to meet some of the girls here. Have you seen Ingrid?"

"I don't think so."

"Well," Miriam said. "I'll join you, but just until they arrive."

As soon as Miriam sat, she started sharing the details of Cheryl's class. Pete seemed captivated. Yet, it wasn't the yoga that had him leaning toward her and listening intently. Though he had never openly admitted it, Pete had always found Miriam a bit enchanting. They first met about a year earlier, after a tennis match in which he and Doug were doubles partners. Doug introduced Miriam and Pete had been surprised to see how attractive and vibrant she was. Doug had led him to believe she was nothing but an overbearing know-it-all. *Miriam never shuts her mouth. Miriam doesn't stop nagging. Miriam thinks she is twenty-five again.* But as Pete sat listening to Miriam, all he could think was how lovely and charming she was. It made him sad that Doug did not recognize or appreciate who she was or what he had.

"Have you ever done yoga?"

"I haven't, but Cheryl keeps telling me it's good for my tennis game."

Miriam spotted Ingrid and some of the others walking into the restaurant. "Oh, Pete," she stood up and waved to her friends. "It's good for so many more reasons than just tennis."

"In that case Miriam, maybe I will make yoga my New Year's resolution."

Miriam clapped her hands. "I am going to hold you to that, Pete Coolidge."

Pete watched her walk away and when he turned back to Jeff, he was met with a curious look.

"What was that?" Jeff said.

"What was what?" Pete felt himself grow defensive, just as the waiter approached with their food.

"I thought I detected . . . something there." Jeff motioned to Pete and to the spot where Miriam had been sitting.

"I have no interest in romance at this point in my life—you know that. Besides," he added, "Miriam is with Doug."

Jeff rolled his eyes. "Yeah, well that's a pairing that's a mystery to everyone. But what do you mean 'at this point in my life'?"

Pete looked away. "We talked about this already."

Jeff felt an impulse to challenge Pete. Though, he knew better. He knew what it was like to live from that place, to feel security and comfort in shutting down that part of yourself once you've lost someone you loved, clinging to your commitment to them even after they're gone. But, for the first time since Jennifer's death, he recognized the true root of that feeling and it wasn't loyalty. It was fear. Fear had convinced Pete, and Jeff for a time, that it wasn't possible to be happy again. When their wives died, fear convinced them that the possibility to love again died as well. But Jeff was beginning to realize giving in to the fear was not a forgone conclusion.

Pete focused on the plate of food in front of him. He'd convinced everyone that he'd succeeded at managing his grief. That he'd created a life without Sally that was everything he could want in her absence. But was he just brushing off feelings and blocking himself from something more? Jeff asking about Miriam had raised something in him, something he'd spent a long time burying. He volleyed the questions back to Jeff.

"What about you? And Kimberly last night?"

Jeff put his drink down. "Kimberly?" As soon as he heard himself say her name, he brightened. A flutter in his stomach told him he knew exactly what Pete was asking, but he wasn't about to admit it. "I met her back in New York. She was friends with Jennifer. Her husband sold me my place here."

Pete nodded, though he too sensed there was something more Jeff wasn't telling him. It wasn't his style to press a difficult conversation, so he ate the last piece of salmon on his plate, put his napkin on the table, and soothed whatever tension was present by replaying the joy of his victory on the court.

* * *

Cheryl was busy in the kitchen planning a farewell lunch for Kimberly—an idea that arose out of nowhere but that she couldn't let go despite Kimberly's protests. The party was the perfect excuse to bring all their friends together. Besides, it was a great opportunity for Cheryl to launch the book she'd been working on for a long time.

During the visit, she'd talked to Kimberly extensively about it. She had written a book about finding love later in life

titled, *Love After*. When she shared the concept with Kimberly, her eyes were wild with enthusiasm.

"We need a book like this, Kimmie."

The "we" Cheryl was referring to were people their age who found themselves unexpectedly single in the later years of their lives. "We have been telling ourselves this story that you only get one great love of your life. It's a myth! It has kept us bound to loveless relationships for far too long for fear of being alone. For others, we lose our first love and close ourselves off to any possibility of finding love again."

Kimberly had smiled and nodded, but she could not comprehend letting herself find love—much less starting over. The idea of dating again, of possibly getting married again, it all seemed harrowing and exhausting. But just because it wasn't for her didn't mean that it wasn't for other people out there. "It's a great idea, Cheryl," Kimberly said, hoping her voice was more encouraging than she actually felt.

"Don't even get me started about self-love. That's not even a phrase in our generation's vocabulary. I am making it my mission to change that too. We can't keep living our lives as if all the ideas we've been fed are the only way. There's so much more to life than we were taught to believe."

Kimberly smiled and nodded, not quite sure of how to respond. She certainly couldn't help but agree that life was rarely what you expected, but she wasn't sure if that was the same idea that Cheryl was fixated on. But she adored her friend and would do anything to support her and her book.

* * *

Cheryl was in full party-planning mode when Kimberly walked into the kitchen to grab her phone. Cheryl was leafing through a pile of catering menus and looked up. "I'm not taking no for an answer. We're doing this."

Kimberly walked out of the kitchen toward the living room.

"If you learned anything being here, Kimmie," Cheryl called after her, "I hope it's that people enjoy doing nice things for people they love."

Kimberly knew better than to argue. When Cheryl wants to do something, she does it. The stubbornness could be a bit much at times, but Kimberly loved Cheryl's tenacity. But it really wasn't the party that made Kimberly uncomfortable. She had come to enjoy the friendships she made in Savannah Valley and the reverie that filled many of her days. Spending time with them would be lovely. Knowing the party signified her return to life in New York—that was the part she dreaded.

"The party will be here," Cheryl announced from inside. "You can just tell me who you want on the guest list."

Kimberly was dialing Jocelyn's number and gestured to Cheryl to keep it down. She walked away to find some privacy. She hadn't spoken to Jocelyn since Christmas Eve.

"Hey, Mom." Jocelyn answered after one ring. "How are you?"

Kimberly sighed. It was nice to hear her daughter's voice. There was always a closeness between them, but since losing Andrew, their bond felt stronger, more imperative.

"Mom, are you there?"

Kimberly took a breath. "Fine. Yes, Jocelyn. Sorry, I was distracted for a second. Tell me about you. How has your holiday been?"

"It was quiet, Mom. No galas for me this year. Just some friends, a nice dinner—low-key just how I wanted it."

"That sounds like how I would have wanted it too," Kimberly said.

"You have had plenty of quiet Christmases. I am glad you went out. I saw the photos—you looked fantastic. You should sneak that dress into your suitcase when you come home."

Kimberly laughed. But even hearing her daughter speak the words, "come home," made her stomach clench. She rubbed the tension in her neck while she listened to Jocelyn talk about the logistics of Kimberly's return. How she had arranged for Cole to pick her up from the airport on the morning of the thirtieth and ideas for what they could do together on New Year's Eve. Then, she noticed a sudden lull in the conversation. Jocelyn stopped talking.

"Joss? Is everything okay?"

There was no response. "Jocelyn?" Kimberly raised her voice a bit. After a pause long enough that it caused Kimberly to check if they had lost connection, she heard Jocelyn sigh.

"I just miss Dad." Jocelyn broke into heaving sobs.

Kimberly hadn't heard Jocelyn cry since the day Andrew died. Her daughter was not emotional—she never had been. She found comfort in maintaining business as usual, taking care of things, making sure all the details were tended to, soldiering on. She was so good at keeping it together, staying

busy. In between sobs, Kimberly heard Jocelyn say, "I am so sorry mom. I am so sorry."

"Oh, honey," Kimberly pressed the phone closer to ear. "I am here." As soon as those words came out of her mouth, she felt a pang of guilt. She wasn't. She wasn't where she should be, where her daughter needed her. She had flown off to another state, to a utopia of her friend's design, leaving Jocelyn to deal with her grief all alone. There was nothing she could do or say to take away her daughter's pain. With the phone still pressed to her ear, she walked outside to the patio. A flock of small birds scattered from a tree just as she opened the sliding glass door and closed it behind her. She stood looking at the clouds overhead until Jocelyn finally settled down. She listened to her daughter's breaths as they slowed.

Kimberly waited with the phone still close to her. She put her hand on her heart and breathed as deeply as she could trying to soothe the pain in her daughter's cries from a distance. Nothing she could say could help her—she knew that. Instead, she closed her eyes and whispered into the phone for Jocelyn to hear, "I miss him too."

* * *

December 28

I have never been so grateful for sleep. To wake in the morning without dread reminding me that I have to face another day, another night alone—this is freedom. I am no longer afraid to open my eyes to life. It's funny how much I have been thinking about what it means

to be strong. Back when climbing a mountain was my biggest challenge to overcome, I thought I was so strong, so capable of enduring even the most strenuous conditions. But nothing compares to the strength I have had to find to navigate this grief. To feel the depths of despair that come with loss. To keep my heart open. To stare into a future I no longer recognize. To take a step forward into the unknown. I am finding a strength I never knew existed.

I have been thinking about Pete. I wish I knew how to pry his heart open. I wish I knew how to take away the fear that is blocking him from truly being whole again. I can see now how people get in their own way from being truly alive. Thank you, Jennifer, for teaching me this lesson. Thank you for the wisdom that will carry me forward into the mystery of what lies ahead. Prayers for dear Kimberly as she moves through these early stages.

"You should stay a little longer," Jeff suggested to Kimberly. It was the first time they saw each other since the gala. Jeff had been urged to reach out to her the next day, but he wanted to give her space. Kimberly, too, had not wanted to reach out. Her mind was already flooded with the angst of going home. Her thoughts of Jeff began to dissipate altogether until the moment he walked into the restaurant where she and Cheryl were finishing lunch. He spotted them first and without hesitation walked over to their table.

Cheryl looked up and smiled. "Well, hello, Jeff Diamond. Fancy meeting you here."

"Hello, Cheryl." His gaze turned to Kimberly. "Hey, Kimberly. How are you doing?"

Kimberly smiled. She felt his sincerity. "I'm doing pretty well, Jeff. Thanks for asking. It's nice to see you."

There was a long silence until Cheryl finally spoke. "Well, I have a meeting with my agent in about ten minutes. Kimberly and I were planning to walk the nature trail, but now I don't have the time. Maybe you can be my replacement, Jeff?"

Kimberly rolled her eyes at Cheryl.

"What? It's just a walk. What's so complicated about a walk?

In fact, Jeff, I am just getting up. Why don't you take my seat?"

Before he could answer, Cheryl gave Kimberly a quick hug and rushed off with her phone in hand. When she was out of sight, Jeff and Kimberly looked at each other.

"So, how about that walk?" Jeff said.

* * *

The trail wound through the densest parts of the forest preserve and opened to a small creek where the two sat on an old tree stump and listened to the quiet rush of a small waterfall in the distance.

Together again, they found themselves opening up more about their experiences since the loss of their spouses. They talked about their marriages, their families. It seemed that no topic was off limits. Kimberly found herself amazed at how

easy it was to talk to Jeff about things she hadn't fully opened up about even to Cheryl. They both cried as they shared the intensity of emotions that had shaped their days, and the deep sadness that had enveloped the nights alone.

"It's crazy to think about how many things I never thought I would do since losing Jennifer."

"Like what?" Kimberly's eyes fell toward a fallen tree in the distance.

Jeff picked up a stick and rustled through the layers of foliage. "I started journaling right after she died. Never in my wildest dreams would I ever consider myself a writer. But journaling became the only place I could go where I wasn't overwhelmed with my thoughts. It's almost become like meditation or prayer for me."

His words reverberated in the silence until Kimberly replied.

"When Andrew died, I tried so hard to turn to my faith. I found myself so lost, so confused, so challenged by faith. Is that awful?"

Jeff stopped playing with the stick and put it back on the ground. "No, it makes perfect sense. Everything you knew and counted on in one day was gone. How can you not question everything you ever believed in?"

Kimberly felt a wave of relief. She had been holding so much guilt and didn't realize it until now. "Jeff, can I ask you something?"

"Of course."

"Have you ever been angry at God?"

Jeff sat back down. "I used to be. When Jennifer got sick, I found myself struggling with God. I prayed hard for a miracle, and when she died, I was furious." He put his fists up to the sky. "Like how could God do this to me? But now, I don't know, I don't feel angry anymore. Something happened when I finally stopped fighting and let myself feel grief instead of running from it. Something I never really understood because—perhaps—I never had to."

Hearing there was something on the other side of pain filled Kimberly with a little hope. They sat for a few minutes, and it was Kimberly who got up first. "Shall we keep going?"

The irony of her question was not lost on Jeff. "Do we have a choice?"

They walked until the path ended and opened to a clearing. The trail ended close to the town square where their once secluded and private walk in the woods gave way to the first sign of who were people out and about. There was an enormous flat patch of green grass in the distance. They headed toward it and when they got there, Kimberly stopped. "Since being here," she said and slipped off her shoes, "I find the one thing that gives me relief is nature—which is strange," she said and tilted her head. "Being in the city for so long, I never realized what I was missing." The grass felt soft beneath her feet. "Just this." She closed her eyes. "Sometimes all I need is just this."

* * *

It was already after three when they parted ways. He made sure to tell Kimberly that he planned on seeing her at the farewell party in two days. He almost admitted how happy he was that he'd see her again before she left, but he resisted. As they hugged goodbye, Jeff felt her whole body lean into his. In that moment, it felt like they were the only two people in the world. She let go first and walked across the field toward the clubhouse to meet Cheryl. She'd skipped away, realizing she was almost a half an hour late.

Jeff had lost himself so fully in their time together, that he hadn't realized he missed several calls from Alex. He waited until she was on the other side of the field to reach for his phone to call his son back.

"Hey, Dad!"

Jeff was happy to hear his voice. "Hey, Alex. It's good to hear from you."

"You, too. How's it going there?"

Jeff slowed his pace and looked around. He spotted Miriam and Pete outside the theater on his walk home. He made sure to keep his distance and took a different route, so they didn't see him. They appeared deep in conversation, and he didn't want to interrupt them.

"It's nice, Alex. It's been really nice." The late afternoon sun made its dip toward the horizon and Jeff squinted as he gazed off into the distance. "This trip has been really good for me." Admitting something felt good was still hard to do. Since Jennifer had died, he'd felt this certainty that the rest of his life wasn't allowed to be okay.

"I'm glad," Alex said. "That's really good for you. I just called to tell you that, sadly, I can't make it there on New Year's."

Jeff stopped a few yards from his road. "Oh? Is everything okay?"

"Everything is fine. Things are just too busy. Even if I were there, I don't think I'd be able to relax. The closing on this deal is so close and I don't want to be distracted until I see it through."

Jeff could almost hear Jennifer's voice: *Alex, there are way more important things in the world than business deals and working.* But saying something like that felt entirely hypocritical. Alex grew up watching Jeff consumed with work. It had taken up almost all of Jeff's time until Jennifer was sick. He wanted to tell Alex that he was sad he wasn't coming. He wanted to tell him how much it would mean if they could spend more time together. Why was it so hard to tell him that? He was just a few blocks away from the house and his throat had tightened. Tears started to arise out of nowhere. "It's okay, Alex. Another time for sure."

"Definitely, Dad." Alex sounded rushed, and Jeff was glad he hadn't detected the disappointment in his father's voice. "Thanks for understanding."

Jeff nodded his head as he approached the circular driveway. "Of course. What else could I do but offer you understanding?"

"We'll get together soon—after things settle down."

As if things ever really settle down. We think there always will be time. Jeff knew these things. He knew this was the truth. But instead of speaking them aloud to his son, he ended the call and went into the house. He felt himself pulled

straight through the house and into the backyard. There, he slipped his shoes from his feet and stepped down onto the lawn. With his eyes closed, he thought of Kimberly and her voice saying, "just this."

A whisper sounded in his ear, "I just wanted to show you that happiness can be found again. Even now."

Perhaps Alex wasn't ready to see that yet, but Jeff was.

CHAPTER FOURTEEN

Farewell Party

*M*iriam stood outside Cheryl's front door with an enormous bouquet of hydrangeas in one hand and a bottle of pink champagne in the other. She cradled the flowers in one arm and rang the bell. "Hello?" She rang again. "Hello? Cheryl, are you there?"

Cheryl was in the kitchen directing the caterer where to put jars of olives and sun-dried tomatoes. The house smelled of fresh basil and tarragon picked from her garden, and one server, dressed in white linen, was busy chopping, as another filled a glass bucket with ice from the freezer. Over the bustle of the noise, Cheryl heard the doorbell.

"The door is open!" she shouted from the kitchen.

Miriam pushed the door with a free hand and came inside. Light bounced into the room and stretched across the wood floor. From where she stood, Miriam caught a glimpse of the backyard. A long picnic table dressed in gingham and vintage China featured prominently on the patio. Glass mason jars of wildflowers and tall candles lined the length of the table, and a band of colored lights were strung overhead. The setting was exactly as Cheryl envisioned it: an elegant picnic. It felt like the perfect setting to celebrate her favorite subject: love.

Cheryl walked out of the kitchen to see Miriam by the front entrance with the flowers and champagne. "These are for you." Miriam handed the flowers to Cheryl and smiled.

"Hydrangeas are my absolute favorite." Cheryl held the blooms to her face.

"They were historically known to be the boastful flower," Miriam said. "And you are someone who deserves to be more boastful for all you do."

"And that must be for us." Cheryl pointed to the champagne.

Miriam followed Cheryl to the kitchen. Setting the flowers gently on the counter, Cheryl looked back at Miriam and said, "You look fantastic."

"Oh, you like it?" Miriam touched the sides of her dark hair. "I decided to go back to my natural color."

"Natural looks good on you." Cheryl winked and reached for a vase on a shelf above the sink. "Is Doug coming?" She was careful to ask.

"I don't want to talk about it."

Cheryl turned off the faucet and approached her friend. "Miriam, we don't have to talk about it. But please know whatever you need, you are supported."

Despite her best efforts to hold back, Miriam began to cry. The fact was, earlier that same day, she had finally found the nerve to tell Doug she wanted to leave him—and this time she meant it.

Miriam and Doug had been together for almost three decades. They had their fair share of conflict and even explored a trial separation years earlier, but they always came back together. Comfort and familiarity kept them in a constant bond of attachment and shared history. The last few

years, though, had been the hardest as Doug struggled with chronic pain and a never-ending negative attitude. Miriam couldn't take it anymore. When Doug arrived home that afternoon, Miriam was waiting by the door dressed for the party.

"Where are you going?" Doug asked as he walked past her toward the kitchen.

This was a moment she had rehearsed in her mind so many times. "I am leaving Doug."

"Leaving where?"

"I am going to Kimberly's party at Cheryl's. And, after that, I am not sure I will be coming home anytime soon."

"The party's tonight?" He didn't acknowledge the rest she had said. He had heard it before. She'd never done it before so he had no reason to think she would actually do it this time.

Miriam closed her eyes and took a deep breath. *Calm down, Miriam. Don't let him see you break down,* she coached herself in her mind.

"I am going to the party alone, Doug." She threw up her hands and steeled her voice. "And I am not coming back."

Doug took out leftovers from the refrigerator and set them on the counter. "I'll believe it when I see it."

Without a word, Miriam grabbed her clutch from the counter and walked out of the house.

When she got in the car, her body was trembling from head to toe. She checked her reflection in the rear-view mirror and fixed the line of smudged mascara. But once the tears had started, they could not be stopped. She knew in her heart the relationship with Doug had ended years ago, but he was

the person with whom she had built a life. Fantasizing about leaving him was a lot easier than actually doing it.

She put the key in the ignition and pulled away from the house. On the drive to Cheryl's, she heard a voice inside her head. "It is never too late to find happiness." Staying in a miserable marriage because of fear of being alone was worse than being alone could ever be. That fear had kept her from truly knowing what she deserved in life. At sixty, she was finally choosing to put her needs over anybody else's, and it was the scariest and most exhilarating choice of her life.

"Can I get you anything?" Cheryl asked pointing to the spread of assorted cheeses and breads arranged on the counter. Miriam wiped the tears from her eyes. She waved her hand. "I can wait."

"Let's not wait for this." Cheryl popped open the champagne and poured two glasses, handing one to Miriam. She held up her glass. "Here's to farewells and how they teach us to appreciate how strong we are."

Miriam closed her eyes in a long blink, focusing on her breaths and what was done was done. She clinked her glass with Cheryl. "To celebrating farewells."

* * *

It was almost four thirty and the party would begin at five. Kimberly was upstairs getting ready and making the final arrangements for her departure the following day. Cole would pick her up and take her straight home. Jocelyn was meeting her at the apartment after work, and the two would have dinner. Kimberly checked the time again—something she had

been doing obsessively since she got up before the sun that morning. It felt like she was counting the minutes she had left in Savannah Valley. It was hard to fathom that the next night she would be sleeping alone in her apartment on Park Avenue.

She slipped her pale-yellow floral dress over her head. The skirt fell to her ankles, and she tied the two long ribbons in the back into loose bows. Kimberly turned around a few times in the mirror and took pleasure in the romantic feel of the sweet dress. She peered closer in the mirror and noticed the heaviness in her face had faded some, though there was still a sadness in her eyes that hadn't changed since the day Andrew died. She wondered how long she would look this way. How long would it take for her spirit to come back? She checked the time on her phone once more before she switched off the light, put her phone on the nightstand, and walked out of the bedroom.

* * *

Jeff and Pete arrived exactly on time, and Kimberly was there to greet them. Pete handed her a bottle of white wine.

"It's great to see you again, Pete," she said, admiring the wine's label. "Thank you for coming."

Pete spotted Miriam out in the backyard. "Thanks for inviting me. I hear this was a very select group."

Kimberly laughed and encouraged Pete to help himself to hors d' oeuvres out back.

As Pete stepped away, Jeff stood waiting in the doorway. The two had not seen each other since their walk.

"It's great to see you again, Kimberly." Jeff handed her a

small paper bag tied with ribbon. "This is fresh mint from my garden."

Kimberly took the package and could smell the hit of mint through the bag. "Cheryl will love this." She looked up. "And it's really nice to see you too, Jeff."

* * *

The women sat across from the men. There was Ingrid, Miriam, and Kimberly on one side, and Vince, Pete, and Jeff on the other. Pete and Miriam were deep in conversation about their New Year's plans. Miriam was reveling in Pete's rapt attention, her moments of panic and sadness from hours earlier almost forgotten.

Cheryl was at the head of the table and once drinks were poured, she stood and clinked her spoon against her glass to gather the table's attention. Cheryl waited for the voices to die down before she spoke. "Welcome, my dearest friends of Savannah Valley. I could not be more delighted to see us yet again around a table celebrating a wondrous night."

The group acknowledged one another with smiles. Kimberly gazed around at the faces of the group and at the beautiful grounds around her—the people and place that had held her these weeks. She was going to miss this.

Cheryl continued, "We are here to honor my friend Kimberly and send her home with all of the positive energy we have for her. Kimberly, we love you. And may the power of love continue to carry you through this next transition. May it carry all of us."

Jeff and Kimberly exchanged a glance, as did Pete and

Miriam. What was unspoken that night was felt through the hearts of these friends who spent hours at that table clinking glasses, enjoying delicious food, and appreciating the opportunity to come together and do what each of them in their own way yearned to do more meaningfully than they ever had—connect.

* * *

At the end of the evening, when the last crumbs of chocolate cake rested on plates and the candles were nearly melted, Cheryl stood again and announced that her new book, *Love After,* was publishing soon and was dedicated to all of them. "Everything that ever happened to me in life was always leading me right here." She held the galley up for everyone to see.

The group applauded, and not a one of them were surprised that Cheryl had done exactly what she'd been saying she would do. She continued to be an inspiration and tireless example of living her truth. Ingrid reached over to inspect the galley more closely.

"What is it about Cheryl?

Cheryl leaned on the table as if she were revealing a secret. "It's about how letting go of everything we thought we knew lets us become available to find the love we are truly meant for and deserve in this life."

In the coming days and months, when Cheryl was in full swing with promotion for her book, she was always asked the same question. "What about you, Cheryl? You left your husband almost twenty years ago. What about finding the love of your life?"

Cheryl perfected her response. She looked the person asking right in the eye and said with the deepest sincerity, "I already have found the love of my life. It took my whole life to find them even though they were always right there." She would be silent for just long enough to be dramatic and conclude, "It was me. The relationship I have with myself is the greatest love of my life."

CHAPTER FIFTEEN

The Phone Call

ole stood outside the town car as Kimberly walked out of the airport terminal. He waved and she tottered toward him, her rollaway suitcase in tow behind her.

"It's good to see you, Kimberly," he said. "This city was not the same without you." He took her suitcase in his hand.

The brisk air hit her skin. "Well, I'm not sure I can say it's good to be back." She shivered. "But I can say it's wonderful to see you." Kimberly slid into the backseat.

Cole shut the door and put her suitcase in the trunk. As he pulled away from the terminal and headed toward the highway, Kimberly put her phone on silent and gazed at the city skyline up ahead.

It was late afternoon when they arrived on Park Avenue. Kimberly stepped outside of the car. The streets were crowded with people in every direction. Heads were down, phones in hands. Cars honked. The noise, which she'd lived in through-out her entire adult life, felt overwhelming and foreign. This hardly felt like home anymore. She stopped at the entrance to her building, exhaled an audible sigh, and continued through the doors and toward the elevator.

The house was spotless. Jocelyn had said she would make sure everything was tidy, but Kimberly wasn't expecting so much to be tucked away, out of sight. Certain photographs

and sentimental gifts from trips taken over the years were no longer on display. Each room felt sanitized of any remnants that could remind her of what she had lost, of what was permanently gone from her life.

She left her suitcase standing by the counter in the kitchen and stepped into the living room. She scanned the plush velvet sofas and the original photography arranged on the soft wallpapered walls. She recalled the many hours she spent with her decorator going over textiles and paint colors and choosing rugs and art and lighting for this room. Back then, these were pressing matters, and she wished for a moment she could be that woman again. Safeguarded by a world she knew. Now, her house felt like a someone else's home. She felt like a stranger.

Her phone rang.

"Hi, Mom." Her daughter's voice was a welcome sound.

"Hi, darling. My goodness, you did so much here."

"I figured it would be hard to come back to all the memories. I didn't do it alone, Mom. You have a full staff waiting to help."

Kimberly was grateful she wasn't there to organize such a project. Cleaning and storing Andrew's personal things must have been an ordeal.

She put her feet up and lay back on the chaise. "What time are you coming by? I can't wait to see you."

"Me too, Mom. I am trying to finish things up at work. It might be later than I thought. Are you okay without me for a few hours?"

It was a hard question for Kimberly to answer honestly. But fatigue hit her hard, and she was too tired to say anything to Jocelyn other than, "That's fine."

* * *

It was dark when she woke up. Her phone must have slipped onto the floor, and when she picked it up, she noticed three missed calls from Jocelyn. There was a voicemail. Kimberly sat up. Her body stiff with exhaustion, her mind fuzzy and disoriented as she listened to the voicemail: "Hey, Mom. I'm so sorry. It's almost eight, and I'm still at work. This was the first chance I've had to call. There's still a lot to wrap up here. I need more time. I promise to be there in the morning. I'll bring bagels and coffee. We can spend the morning catching up and finalizing our New Year's plans. I hope you are getting rest. See you tomorrow. I love you."

Kimberly checked the time. It was almost ten. She had no idea how long she had been sleeping, and she could barely process her disappointment in not seeing Jocelyn until the next day. She was alone in the house on her first night back and the familiar waves of grief hit her before she could take a breath. Her eyes filled with tears, her chest tightened, and there she was again—gripped by the reality of loss. "No, please. I don't want to feel this way anymore," she called out to the empty room.

She stumbled her way upstairs holding onto the banister. When she got to the top of the landing her heart dropped. How am I going to face this night? She threw herself on her empty bed and lay there waiting for the sobs to subside.

The house was so quiet she could hear the tick of the grandfather clock downstairs. She grabbed a tissue from her nightstand and waited until the next wave of cries erupted, making her writhe and wail. *I can't do this. I can't do this anymore.*

In a fit of prayer and desperation, she reached for her phone. She held it up to her face and scrolled through the names until she found his—Jeff Diamond. She thought of the note he gave her the night of the gala. If there were anyone in the world who would be able to understand how she felt it would be him. She pulled up his number and texted him the only message she could think to write: "I hate this." She knew he would know what she meant.

***

December 30

> *Today, as I struggle to find the same enthusiasm I have been blessed to discover since arriving in Savannah Valley, I thought I should spend time listing the things I am grateful for. I want this list to remind me of the little things that are so easy to forget when my mind contracts and fills with worry, a loop that tells me I am alone.*

> *Things I am grateful for:*

> 1. *My friendship with Pete and for the ways I can tell he is opening up to new ways of living.*
> 2. *My body that is still able to run a few miles, play*

three sets of tennis, and at the end of the day, not be
as stiff as it used to be.

3. *The air of this place. Just walking around, I am*
   reminded of how important it is to breathe in the
   simple surroundings.

4. *Meeting Kimberly.*

Jeff was on the phone with Alex when Kimberly's text came through. Alex was able to clear a few days and would be visiting Jeff in Savannah after the new year holiday. This news soothed the melancholy Jeff felt ever since Kimberly left for New York.

Though they didn't spend much time together, it was hard to get her out of his mind. No amount of tennis or gardening or journaling would quell the longing. Was his heart really ready for connection? He started to think so, though he knew Kimberly was still so early in her grieving. He wanted to be careful.

As soon as he hung up with Alex, he pressed the text message and read her words. *I hate this.* He knew instantly what she meant. Those nights alone were the worst. He texted her back. "Do you want to talk?"

For a flash, he felt like he was messaging a girl from school he had a crush on. It felt juvenile, but exciting. The burst of energy was a welcome arrival. Her text response came through instantly: "Yes."

He dialed her number and when she picked up and heard

his voice, she broke down. "Oh, Kimberly, I am here." He held the phone close to his ear and soothed her as best he could. "Can you hear my voice? I am right here."

"I miss you," Kimberly kept repeating. Her whole body was leaning into the phone as if that would bring his physical presence closer to her. "I miss you."

Jeff was overwhelmed with emotion and the tenderness he felt toward her. He listened to her share about her first night home, the house, Jocelyn, and the terrifying truth that her life will never be the same again. He stared up at the wall thinking of ways he could support her.

"Is there a way you can come back to Savannah Valley? My son is coming into town in a few days, I would love you to meet him. And even more than that, Kimberly, I would love for you to come back. I would love to spend more time together."

His words were a comfort in her otherwise dark night, and by the time they got off the phone, she had agreed that a trip back was a good idea. Why not? She would talk to Jocelyn in the morning, which was the only thing in that moment that gave her cause for concern.

CHAPTER SIXTEEN

Love's Truth

imberly was brewing coffee when Jocelyn walked in, carrying groceries. "Mom! It's so good to see you!" She placed the bags on the counter, turned to her mother, and wrapped her arms around her. Jocelyn rested her head on Kimberly's shoulder like she had done when she was a little girl. Kimberly stroked her hair.

"It's good to see you too, honey. I missed you."

"Are you hungry?" Jocelyn released herself from her mom's arms and got busy unpacking bagels and containers of cream cheese, smoked salmon, and fresh juice.

Kimberly grabbed plates and silverware and set the table. They sat down and both sighed at the same time.

Jocelyn broke the silence between them. "Happy New Year's, Mom." She held up a small tumbler of orange juice.

"Happy New Year's to you." Kimberly tapped her coffee mug to Jocelyn's glass. They talked about going to a film at Lincoln Center, about grabbing sushi before the city got crazy with New Year's revelers. "That all sounds perfect. I can't remember the last time I stayed up past midnight anyway."

Jocelyn's eyes widened. "Mom, do you remember the time you and dad surprised me in Aruba? That was definitely after midnight, and as I'm sure you can recall, I wasn't alone."

"Oh, my goodness! That's right! What was that, three

years ago? I will never forget the look at your dad's face. He wanted to punch that guy. What was his name?"

"Griffin, Mom. His name was Griffin. Dad knew him. He worked for him at one point or something."

Kimberly smiled as she recalled that weekend in Aruba—the awkwardness and the joy. "What happened to Griffin, anyway?"

"Just life." Jocelyn sighed. "He reached out to me when Dad died. We caught up a bit and he asked me out for dinner. I told him I would think about it and let him know."

"Have you?" Kimberly asked, sipping coffee and watching her daughter's face.

Jocelyn looked away. "No. I just don't know anymore. I don't feel ready to connect with anybody. I've been so distracted. I think I just need more time."

Her own daughter had the discipline to hold back from attaching herself to a man right now—how would she understand Kimberly's interest in another man so soon?

Jocelyn sensed that something was off. "I know that look in your eyes. What aren't you telling me?"

Kimberly knew not to lie to her daughter, especially now when she deserved the truth. She put her coffee down and let out a deep breath. "Jocelyn, there is so much I want to tell you. I just don't know where to begin."

They walked to the living room and sat down together. Kimberly took her daughter's hand. "Joss so much has changed. I have changed. I need to figure out a way I can move forward with my life now." She looked around the

room and then closed her eyes. "I am not sure I can do that staying here."

Jocelyn stared. "What does that mean? You haven't even been home twenty-four hours and you're ready to leave again? You need to give yourself some time here at home."

How could Kimberly explain to her daughter that this no longer felt like her home? "It's more than giving things time. Time won't bring back what life was before—"

"Of course, it won't," Jocelyn interrupted. "That's not what I was saying."

"There were people in Savannah Valley who helped me see so much about myself and my life—things I never realized before. Even the little time I spent there, I started to see my life through a totally different lens."

"I don't understand."

"I wasn't ready to come back. And after New Year's, I'd like to return to Savannah for a longer stretch of time. Maybe a few months."

Jocelyn's face contracted. "Months?"

Kimberly nodded. "It's just a flight away, Jocelyn. You can come visit me anytime. Coming back here felt wrong. I need to be moving forward."

Jocelyn stood up, as if to leave the room.

"Joss, don't walk away. Stay with me. We have to talk about this and deal with. I know it's uncomfortable."

"Don't tell me about dealing with things. You are the one who wants to run away. Savannah Valley was a vacation. This is your real life."

Instead of defending herself and snapping at Jocelyn, who seemed more concerned about controlling her life than taking care of her own, Kimberly paused. She heard Cheryl's words inside her head. Live your truth. Despite Jocelyn's protests, Kimberly pressed on.

"Also, Joss, and I know this is not going to be easy for you to hear. When I was there, I connected with someone. A man. He has been a good friend to me. His own wife died over a year ago."

Jocelyn interrupted her. "Are you kidding me? Dad just died. You are already moving on? You can't be alone for more than a month? How could you do that to Dad? He was your husband. We are your family. How could you do that to us?"

Jocelyn's words were a punch to Kimberly's gut. "I am not doing anything to you or to your dad. For the first time in my life, I am listening to myself. I am doing something for me. Don't I get a chance to do that, especially now? I would want the same for you."

Jocelyn put her head in her hands. The thought of mother moving on so soon was too much for her to accept. "It's just not right, Mom. He hasn't even been gone two months. How could you even think about someone else?"

"I don't know." Kimberly stood up. "There's so much I didn't know. There's still so much I don't know. I want to be happy and live again. I can't spend the rest of my life holding vigil for your father. What kind of life would that be? Would he want that?"

"Don't do that, Mom. That isn't fair. Dad isn't here

anymore to tell you what he would want. You can't put words into his mouth."

"If I knew anything about your father, I know that he would want me—us—to find happiness again."

Jocelyn struggled to process what was happening. She'd already had to say goodbye to her father. She couldn't imagine saying goodbye to her mother as well. Her family was crumbling in her hands.

Kimberly walked to her and put her hands on her shoulders. "Jocelyn, there is no guarantee in this life that things will work out the way we want them to—no matter how much we try to control and plan. I loved your father so very much. We had a beautiful life, but that life is over. That doesn't mean I want to forget the life I shared with your father. The day he died, my life changed forever. I can look at that as an opportunity to change or I can cling to what I had that is gone. If I leave New York, that doesn't mean I'm leaving you."

Jocelyn nodded and stepped away. She went into the kitchen and began filling the dishwasher. Kimberly followed and began putting the food away. Soon, the kitchen was clean and the dishes were done.

"When will you leave?" Jocelyn rinsed the sponge under the water.

"After New Year's."

Jocelyn turned off the water and rested the sponge on the counter. "I need time to process this, Mom."

Kimberly detected the slightest softness in her daughter's voice. She took that as good sign and nodded her head. "Of

course, Jocelyn. Of course, it's going to take time." She moved closer to her. "And sometimes it takes more than letting time pass for things to feel different."

CHAPTER SEVENTEEN

*O*n a Sunday in Savannah Valley, Jeff waited outside the clubhouse for Alex to arrive. He spotted a black town car and waved as Alex climbed from the back-seat. Jeff walked toward him with his arms stretched wide.

"Alex!" Jeff smiled. "Look at you! You look good for someone who barely leaves his office." They embraced and Jeff pulled away, gazing at his son. "I mean it, Alex. You look good."

"You look good, too, Dad. But I would expect nothing less from someone who skipped town to live in paradise." He turned to take in the landscape. "Look at this place."

The sky was crystal clear, and the sun beamed overhead. "I requested this weather especially for you," Jeff said.

Alex slung his bag over his shoulder and reached for his sunglasses. "I appreciate that, Dad. I will let you know the next time I need fresh powder on the slopes."

Jeff had his arm over his shoulder as they made their way to the clubhouse for lunch. When they reached the restaurant, they bumped into Pete and Miriam who were just leaving.

"What a small world!" Pete approached Jeff and Alex at the entrance and shook Alex's hand.

"Pete! I barely recognized you off a tennis court, wearing something other than your whites. How are you?"

Having never had kids of his own, Pete had always held a deep affection for Alex. "Look at you! All grown up and running the show." They smiled at one another. Pete remembered Miriam next to him and took her hand. "As for me? I'd say I have never been better. This is Miriam."

"Nice to meet you, Miriam." Alex furrowed his brow, unsure of how to take the introduction.

Miriam held out her hand. "Likewise, Alex. I have heard so much about you. And, might I say," she said standing back and surveying Jeff and Alex, "the two of you could be brothers."

"Yeah? Which is the older brother?" Jeff mused.

Miriam shook her head. "It's not about how old you are anymore gentlemen. It's about how old you feel." With that, she took Pete's hand.

"See you tomorrow on the court," Pete called, as Miriam pulled him away. "Assuming I survive Cheryl's sunset yoga, of course!"

Jensen arrived just then. "Happy new year, gentlemen."

"Happy new year, Jensen. Table for two, please?"

"Of course, Mr. Diamond. You must be the other 'Mr. Diamond,'" Jensen shook Alex's hand. "I have a table ready in the back by the window."

"Thank you, Jensen." They followed him through the restaurant to their table. Alex waited for Jensen to hand them menus and take their drink orders before he asked, "What is going on with Pete?"

Jeff looked up from the menu. "Oh, you mean Pete and Miriam?"

Alex nodded. "I mean Pete and Miriam—and Pete and yoga? What goes on around here, Dad?"

Jeff laughed.

"I mean it. This place feels so—" Alex struggled to find the right word.

"For me, it feels like home," Jeff said.

Alex scanned the tables, filled with people so relaxed and content on a midweek afternoon. It was a stark contrast to life back in New York, where the relentless pace left him in a constant state of never having enough time.

The drinks arrived just as Jeff's phone rang. Ordinarily, he would not pick up during their meal, but it was Kimberly. He was expecting her to arrive the day of Alex's departure and they were still finalizing details. "Excuse me, Alex. I have to take this." Jeff stood from the table and found a private spot around the corner to take the call.

"Kimberly, how are you?"

"I just wanted to let you know that I am all set. I thought about your invitation to stay with you, and since Cheryl is busy with the book, I think I'll do it." She beamed into the phone. "Is that still okay?"

He immediately felt his face crack into a wide smile and tried to keep his voice level. "That's great news, Kimberly. I promise, you'll feel right at home. I am just sitting down to lunch with Alex, so I will call you later."

He walked back to the table, trying to seem low-key while bursting with excitement inside.

"Who was that?" Alex said grabbing a piece of fresh bread from the basket on the table.

"That was Kimberly, Kimberly Langley in New York."

"Do I know her?" Alex picked up his butter knife.

"I don't think so. She was a friend of your mom's." Jeff paused before continuing, "And, recently, she has become a really good friend of mine as well."

Their lunch arrived and Alex waited for the waiter to leave them alone before he asked.

"A friend? The look on your face says otherwise."

Jeff was reluctant to tell him the whole truth—a truth that in the last few days had been increasingly clearer. Since the day he saw Kimberly at the gala, something within him had shifted. It certainly had been unexpected, but the more he spoke to Kimberly, the more he thought about her, the more something awakened within his heart. He knew he was falling in love. Now that Jennifer was gone, he felt like their entire life was preparing him this next phase of life and love. But he had no idea how to explain that to his son.

"Since I've been talking to Kimberly . . . I'm feeling things I haven't felt since your mom—except this is different. Maybe it's because I am older. Maybe it's because I never thought this would happen to me again—"

"What is it, Dad?"

"I am in love, Alex. I am in love with Kimberly." As soon as Jeff said the words out loud, he knew how true they were.

"Love, Dad? Isn't that a little fast? I mean what about Mom? Don't you still love her?"

"Your mother will always be a great love of my life. That will never change."

"So, what are you saying? That there is more than just one love of your life?"

"I don't know, Alex. Are their rules about these things? When I lost your mother, I never thought I would ever be this happy again. But Kimberly makes me happy. I want you to meet her. I want you to see for yourself what I mean."

Alex pushed away from the table, absorbing this unexpected news. He stared at his father. For most of his life, Alex had watched his dad dominate every obstacle, achieve every goal. He was an admired leader Alex hoped to emulate. But since his mother had gotten sick, he'd watched his father shrink smaller and smaller within himself. He'd watched him lose the passion and drive he had always possessed.

He couldn't help but worry this was moving too fast, this was impulsive and reckless and could potentially hurt the man he loved most. As much as the thought of his father with a woman who wasn't his mother, Alex couldn't help but feel relieved. In just the few minutes since his father had talked to Kimberly, the life had come back into his father's eyes, the passion was returning to his voice. He believed his father would always love his mother—there was no denying she'd been the great love of his life. But if his father was reawakening to love and wanted Alex to support him, there was no way Alex was letting him down.

"Of course, Dad. I can't wait to meet her."

CHAPTER EIGHTEEN

Return to Love

imberly called Cheryl on the way to the airport. "Finally," she said. "I have been trying to call you for two days. Did you get my messages?"

Cheryl's yearlong book tour was in full swing. Every weekend she would be in a different state, making a new appearance, giving another talk. *Love After* was boasting incredible sales, topping best-seller lists in self-help and nonfiction.

"I am so sorry, Kimmie. It's been one thing after another. This is the first time I had a chance to sit down. I waited to call you, but not until I had the time to really talk." Cheryl was by the pool at the Beverly Hilton in Los Angeles, enjoying some down time in between interviews and events.

Kimberly knew Cheryl would be on the road for the next year. But she was so proud of her. "A bestseller! You never cease to amaze me, Cheryl. But I am not surprised."

Cheryl brushed it off. She didn't want to talk about her. She wanted to hear about Kimberly. "Enough about me. Is it true? Are you on your way back to Savannah Valley now?"

Cole followed the signs for the terminal. They were close. Kimberly smiled. "It's true. I knew I had to come back. It was too hard to resist what was calling me there."

"Now I am the one who is not surprised." Cheryl stretched her legs out on the chaise. "I am so proud of you, Kimmie, for

listening to your heart. It's not always easy or convenient to do that. How is Jocelyn?"

Kimberly sighed, thinking of Jocelyn's tears that morning. "It's going to take a little time for her to understand. She will come around. I know, too, that she wants me to be happy."

"That she does. She loves you and knows you love her. In the end, that's all that matters. She'll see how happy Savannah—and all who are there—make you."

Cole pulled into the departure terminal. "You have a key to the house, Kimmie. You can stay in my bedroom. Mi casa es su casa, as you know. Unless, of course, a certain someone has beat me to the punch? After all, if he's opening his heart to you, he might as well open his door."

"I'm at the airport, Cheryl, so I have to go. Yes, my plan is to stay with Jeff. And the rest of the plan is . . . that I have no plan. I'm just focused on living my best life."

"Listen to you, Kimmie." Cheryl smiled as she put her sunglasses on her head. "Spoken like a true wise soul."

Cole opened the door and Kimberly exhaled into the phone before she stepped out of the car. "All these years it took me to understand what you meant when you said to trust your soul and listen to your heart. For the first time, I think I am starting to understand love in ways I never have before."

Cheryl spotted someone she knew walking toward her and held up a hand to communicate she would be just one minute. "As I have always believed, Kimmie, love is and always will be our greatest teacher in this life."

* * *

On Alex's last morning, Jeff woke him early to hike. A few days in Savannah Valley had rejuvenated Alex, and Jeff was pleased to take care of him in ways he hadn't been able to in so long. Gray clouds hung low in the sky as they made their way to the opening of the trail. It was the first cloudy day Jeff could remember since his arrival in Savannah, which now felt like lifetimes ago.

Alex eyed the clouds. "Looks like rain."

"The trees are nature's umbrella." Jeff touched a tall oak that divided the trail. "Let's take the long route. We have time."

Except for the crunch of the dried leaves underneath their feet, the woods were silent. "When I first arrived, I came here almost every day and prayed." They walked to the creek where Jeff and Kimberly had talked.

Alex knelt and sifted through the ground for stones. He tossed a small one into the creek. The splash echoed and the rain began to tap against the thick, leafy canopy overhead.

"I can see why you like this place so much, Dad. I am glad I came."

"Me too, Alex. Me too." Jeff walked a little further down the path until he stopped and watched Alex walk toward him. "You remind me so much of your mother, you know."

Alex looked surprised. "Really? Everyone always says I am so much like you."

"Well, maybe you look like me, and you unfortunately inherited my career ambition." Jeff smiled. "But after your mother died, every time I saw you, I couldn't help but think of her. At first that was unbearable because, God, I missed her so

much. But now, when I see you, I see her and all I feel is love in my heart."

Alex felt the sting of tears burning his eyelids. It had been a long time since he let himself cry.

"Your mom would only want the very best for both of us. You know that don't you, Alex? She wouldn't want us to waste our time pining for what we could no longer have. She wouldn't want you to be chasing life away hiding behind paperwork and scoring the next big deal. She would want you to be the happiest you can be in this life. And I want that for you too."

Alex could no longer hold in his tears, and they gave way to heavy sobs. Jeff held him close, thinking how long it had been since he'd held his son like this. "The best gift we can give your mom is to be happy."

Jeff held Alex's face between his hands and looked him in the eyes. "I know these years haven't been easy."

Alex wiped his tears with the back of his hand. "I've been fighting these feelings for so long. I have been avoiding feeling this." He exhaled. "And, yet, in feeling this grief," he beat his hand against his chest, "I can see how it opens me to some-thing bigger. I just didn't want to feel it because it hurts so much."

"I know it does Alex." Jeff held him for a long time. A year ago, he wouldn't have been able to. A year ago, he was barely able to hold himself. Just then, a soft breeze rustled through the leaves. The air touched their skin and Alex settled a bit.

"Do you feel that?" Another breeze came through.

Alex closed his eyes. "Yes. I feel it."

"That's her. She's here with us. She's always here." He pointed to his heart.

The air became very still. The woods themselves felt motionless as father and son stood suspended in the love they had for each other, and in the love they were finally learning to give to themselves.

* * *

There was just enough time for Jeff to arrange an early dinner so Alex could meet Kimberly. He waited by the front door while Alex packed upstairs. Before she even had a chance to knock, Jeff opened the door and caught Kimberly on the verge of tears. A momentum had brought them both to this moment—a wave they had both been riding since the day they saw each other at the gala. It was impossible to believe she was here with him. They looked in each other's eyes and without saying a word, they both knew. She dropped her bag, moved toward him, and he wrapped his arms around her.

He whispered into her ear, "I am so happy."

"I am so happy, too," she whispered back.

Alex walked downstairs holding his bag and waved his free hand. "You must be Kimberly Langley—the woman my father cannot stop talking about."

Kimberly blushed. "And you must be Alex, the handsomer, younger version of your father."

"Dad," Alex said, waking toward them and extending his hand to Kimberly, "you forgot to mention how perceptive she is."

Jeff smiled and stepped out of the way so Kimberly and Alex could shake hands.

Rather than take his hand, however, Kimberly surprised herself and opened her arms. "How about a hug?"

Alex obliged and Kimberly stood on her tip toes to reach her arms around his shoulders. Whatever awkwardness might have been there was dispelled. They sat down at the table together, shared a meal, and talked. The conversation was smooth and engaging, and when Alex went into the kitchen while clearing the plates, Kimberly had a chance to comment about how much Alex reminded her of him. Jeff smiled.

"I just hope when you meet my daughter she is as ingratiating."

Jeff leaned closer toward her. "However, she will be fine. Besides, she might surprise you. There's just something that happens to people when they are in the presence of true love."

Alex came out of the kitchen. A car would be waiting for him outside soon. Kimberly rose from her chair.

"Alex, it was so nice to meet you. I look forward to seeing you again."

Jeff put his arm around Alex. "Isn't she everything I said she was?"

Kimberly was amazed at how comfortable and open Jeff was in expressing his feelings with Alex. For a moment, she worried if this was all too much and too soon—for both Alex and Jocelyn.

"She is great Dad. But I wouldn't expect anything less. You have always had great taste in women."

Kimberly appreciated the comment and also knew underneath it was Alex's protection of his mother. She thought of Jocelyn's request to give her more time. Even if Jeff was ready to burst into a full-blown celebration, Kimberly respected that their family and friends might need time to catch up to them and their excitement.

Jeff walked Alex to the front door and the two embraced for a long time until there was the sound of a car outside.

"Thanks, Dad, for a great visit. I loved it."

"May there be many more of these days ahead of us, son."

"I will remember that the next time I turn down an opportunity to have a good time."

"Well, if I taught you anything Alex, it's that there won't always be another opportunity. Take them when they arrive."

Alex looked around the house. He smiled. "You have taught me a lot more than that, Dad. I love you."

"I love you, too, Alex."

Jeff stayed at the window, watching as the car made its way down the driveway and onto the road. He stayed watching until it was out of sight. Kimberly came from the kitchen, and when he turned around, he felt like the luckiest man in the world.

CHAPTER NINETEEN

Jeff & Kimberly

January

The kiss was everything I imagined it would be, and yet it was familiar and comfortable too. I had no idea I would ever feel the excitement of first love like I did when I was young. This first love is so much richer. I am no longer a boy who has no idea what he's doing. I am a man with wisdom and experience, who still sometimes has no idea what he's doing, but I can recognize what I have. Second love is by no means second place. I can hold this love and appreciate it and take care of it. I know it might not be here tomorrow but it's here now and that is enough. What a way to live—what a way to love.

In the days and weeks after Alex left, whenever Kimberly heard the front door open and Jeff call out, "I'm home!" her heart would lurch with joy. His first priority was always to seek her out and wrap his arms around her—whether she was in the kitchen cooking dinner or on the phone in the living room or resting in the backyard reading. Every moment they had was precious and they both knew all too well that tomorrow was not a guarantee. Each day they woke up in each other's arms they acknowledged what a gift it was to have each other.

Kimberly and Jeff were well aware of the rumors and the gossip—the people who would rather dive into their disapproval than accept someone's happiness.

"They are in denial."

"Nobody falls in love that fast."

"It's just a rebound, and it will never last."

But their bliss protected them. Not only were they immune to the sting of such judgment, but they knew the source these opinions came from. Instead, they chose to try to empathize with the naysayers. After all, at one time, they too might not have believed they could have ever opened their hearts so soon after enduring such loss.

Jeff and Kimberly's happiness was infectious to those who loved and supported them. They heard about beautiful new relationships forming among their friends, and many older ones reviving. No longer did they keep their love a secret to protect others or themselves from judgment. Jeff had lived long enough to know he was not responsible for managing other people's feelings, and while Kimberly was more discerning about showing her feelings for Jeff in public, she couldn't help but come around quickly. She was the happiest she had ever been before, and she couldn't hide it anymore.

By the early spring when the grounds of Savannah Valley were ripe with new growth, Jocelyn called and Jeff picked up the phone. Instead of Jocelyn bypassing an opportunity to talk with Jeff by asking for her mother, she stayed on the phone. Jeff was the first to learn that Jocelyn had met someone. He was the first to hear that she had recently fallen in love, and it was Jeff who suggested they plan to come to Savannah Valley before the summer.

In the absence of Cheryl who had a way of breathing love

into the air no matter where she was, Jeff and Kimberly's union seemed to be as strong of an influence on their closest friends. Pete and Miriam were buying a home together. Ingrid and Vince had decided to renew their wedding vows after forty-five years of marriage, inviting everyone to their "celebration of love."

On the day of the Ingrid and Vince's party, Jeff opened his eyes before his alarm went off. Kimberly was still asleep nestled in his arms, and he gazed out the window and watched the sun rise above a span of feathery clouds. It was barely six in the morning. His tennis game was in less than an hour. Kimberly had plans to meet with Miriam to find a gift for Ingrid and Vince a few hours after that. Jeff shifted his body, and she opened her eyes, squinting at the ray of light coming in from the window.

"We have to get up already?" She moaned and buried her head against his chest.

"Soon, my love," he said, and he reached for his phone.

Kimberly thought about the day ahead and the hours they would spend apart from one another. She regretted all the commitments she made. He too sighed at the thought of getting up and saying goodbye. He didn't want to leave. She didn't even want to even say "see you later."

She reached for her phone and shook her head at all the commitments she'd made for the day. She turned to Jeff and he to her, and they read each other's minds. Then, they did something they never would have done in their past lives. They canceled all their plans, put the phones away, and gave

progressing at all in his journey of grief, acceptance, and moving forward into his new life without his life-long love.

But when Russ heard of Mona's loss, he was immediately cast back to the day of his own loss and was astonished to discover he'd actually come a long way.

Initially, it was Russ's friendship for Mona's husband (they'd been friends for years) which motivated him to extend an offer to "be there" for Mona. He knew exactly how devastatingly lonely and discouraging life after loss can be.

At first Mona was grateful, but was so caught up in the chaos of dealing with family, business and estate issues, she was too busy and too numb to realize how wounded she was. And even when she did, she didn't want to burden Russ or anyone else with her sadness.

It took three months, but eventually the cry for help came via the "I hate this" text which we worked into the *Love After* story. This began a conversation about the pain of loss and how to find a way forward. These intimate conversations started out as two friends helping each other through a difficult time, but soon cultivated a romantic interest neither of us thought was possible and certainly weren't seeking.

But there we were . . . in the gravitational pull of love!

We were scared, not sure how to act, what was proper, cautious about ruining our friendship, and worried about hurting our children and being judged harshly by friends and family who might not be ready for either of us to have a new love.

In fact, at first, we weren't even sure if what was happening was love at all.

Were we "rebounding" . . . hiding from our individual sad realities . . . using each other to recreate what we'd lost? These are all valid questions . . . things we needed to think about and discuss honestly. But they forced us into what's become a very fun and intimate dynamic of candor and trust.

We expect even if you've read this far, you're less interested in the details of our story than some of the biggest epiphanies of our journey. So we'll close by simply summarizing those we found the most profound, surprising and helpful.

Survivor's Guilt is Real . . . and Unfair

Both our spouses had their lives cut short through illnesses and a medical system which failed them. As survivors, we each struggle with wondering why we lived, and they didn't. We both feel like we could have done more to help our late spouses survive.

The injustice and second-guessing feeds a subliminal but very strong feeling of being undeserving of happiness . . . or even life itself. It can be very intense.

Of course, there's nothing we can do about the past except learn from it and work to be better going forward. We both did the best we could. And even if mistakes were made, there's no replays, so we must accept the situation and forgive ourselves.

It's easy to say, but hard to do.

Thankfully, we each had very specific experiences we consider to be divine messages which helped free us from our guilt. These were the basis for the "stone" experience Jeff Diamond had in the story.

But whether you have such an experience yourself, it's important to find a way to accept the gift your life is . . . even though it's taken a very difficult turn. There are new joys to discover.

Falling in Love is Also Real . . . and Exhilarating

Each of us built a powerful and enduring love with our late spouses over decades. We both assumed it wouldn't be possible to repeat that process this late in life. Therefore, the notion we'd ever have another "forever love" seemed unrealistic. It seemed we were both destined to either live alone . . . or settle for less with someone new.

What we've discovered is that a big part of the love we'd established with our late spouses over decades was made up of who they were, who we were, and the experiences we'd shared with them along the way.

When our spouses passed, we found that who we'd become individually in those relationships remained. After four decades of marriage each, we'd both become practitioners of "forever love". As we saw this in each other, we found ourselves being drawn together very quickly.

At first, we couldn't accept it. It seemed too good to be true. Guilt crept in and from time to time as one or both of us would feel like our love dishonored our late spouses and that we didn't deserve so much happiness.

Other times, we were giddy with happiness . . . like two high school sweethearts discovering love for the very first time and wondering, "How could this be real?"

But we've been careful not to sabotage a good thing and have adopted a mantra of "accept, enjoy and be grateful" as we continue to take it one day at a time.

You're Qualified to Have an Opinion . . . Keep it Real

When you get married as a very young adult, you really don't understand the totality of the commitment you're making. How can you? The only way you can truly understand what it takes to be faithfully married for four decades is to do it.

Today, we're both entering into our love together with the tremendous benefit of decades of real-world experience. We know what forever love is . . . what it takes to be married for decades. And we know ourselves better than at any other time in our lives.

So, if you're a seasoned citizen facing a new life and love, we encourage you to give yourself credit for experience. You're wiser than you realize.

If you're younger, it might be a good idea to seek out wisdom from older couples who've made it work in good times and bad, in sickness and in health . . . even those who got all the way to "'til death do you part".

For us, love represents something permanent and enduring . . . the glue which keeps you together through all the trials of life. It provides an intimate companionship that helps you feel both valued and connected.

We both lost our forever lovers, but not our desire for forever love. We didn't think we could ever have it again, but trusted our own judgement enough to explore the possibilities when we saw in each other someone who looked at love the way we did.

Curiosity is the Cure and Humor is Healing

Apart from the tremendous sorrow and grief at the time of loss and its wake, we faced an almost debilitating fear and anxiety about a new and uncharted future without the loves of our lives.

Drawing upon lessons learned early in his business career, Russ chose to adopt the attitude of an intrepid explorer . . . someone intensely curious and eager to trek into the jungle of an unimagined life and future to see what's out there.

No guarantees or guidelines. Just an adventure into strange new life . . . each of us without our lifelong companions. This attitude has made the entire journey not only possible, but fun and exciting.

So we've discovered the cure to our fear of the unknown is simple curiosity.

Humor is also essential. We find ourselves laughing at the many awkward phases of learning how to be raw and real with someone completely new. If we didn't, we'd probably be too uptight and self-conscious to develop the deep level of trust and comfort we both long for.

So, we simply explore and laugh . . . and it's made our journey into love after loss a joy so far.

We hope our experiences and insights help you find more joy, love and hope in your journey . . . no matter how the circumstances of your life play out.

May God bless you richly.

It's Review Time

Please leave a review. It would mean the world to us. We want to share possibilities of the joy in life that love after a tragedy can mean to so many. The more people know about this book, maybe, they too can find *Love After*.

Good or bad, we want to hear from you. All it takes is one little sentence, more is good too. We just want to know if you enjoyed our book.

https://www.amazon.com/Love-After-Dreams-Still-Come-ebook/dp/B0BC2H67FT/

ABOUT THE AUTHORS

RUSSELL GRAY

Russ proposed to his high-school girlfriend Cheri when he was just 17 years old. They married three months after graduating, raised a large family, and rode the roller-coaster of life, entrepreneurship, and her fatal battle with cancer. Their love story ended when Cheri died in his arms after 41 years of marriage.

Today, Russ remains a businessman, father, and grandfather. He enjoys studying history, economics, and exploring his new life and love with Mona.

MONA GUARINO

Mona grew up in upstate New York, where in high school she met Gene, the man who would later become her husband of 36 years. They began their family, moved to Arizona to help plant a church, where they had their fourth and final child and launched two successful businesses. Sadly, Gene died unexpectedly after a short, but severe illness.

Today, Mona and her children own and operate the family businesses. She loves being a mother and grandmother, treasures time with her many friends, and is grateful for God's grace and love through her most difficult challenges

Mona enjoys retreats to the mountains, hiking, homemaking, and building a new and wonderful life with Russ.

www.ingramcontent.com/pod-product-compliance
Lightning Source LLC
Chambersburg PA
CBHW060647260626
47161CB00008B/3038